The Barefoot Book of
Ballet Stories

Written by **Jane Yolen** and **Heidi E. Y. Stemple**
Illustrated by **Rebecca Guay**

Barefoot Books
Celebrating Art and Story

For my five granddaughters so they can keep on their toes — J. Y.
For Sandra, who reminds me to dance with life every day — H. E. Y. S.

For my loving husband Matthew, who makes everything possible — R. G.

Barefoot Books
2067 Massachusetts Ave
Cambridge, MA 02140

First published in the United States of America in 2004 by Barefoot Books, Inc.
This hardcover edition published in 2009

This book has been printed on 100% acid-free paper

Graphic design by Barefoot Books, UK
Color separation by Grafiscan, Verona
Printed and bound in China by Printplus Ltd

This book was typeset in Garamond
The illustrations were prepared in watercolor and acryla-gouache on watercolor paper

ISBN 978-1-84686-262-5

7 9 8 6

Library of Congress Cataloging-in-Publication Data is available under LCCN 2004004661

Contents

Coppélia: The Girl with the Enamel Eyes
INTRODUCTION

Coppélia is ballet's most famous and best-loved storybook comedy. Set in a Polish village at the end of the eighteenth century, the ballet is based on a fairy tale by E. T. A. Hoffman, written two hundred years ago. Ernst Theodor Amadeus Hoffman, a German author born in 1776, wrote many fantasy stories, which were often eerie and sinister. Several of Hoffman's tales have been made into great ballets, the most famous of which are *Coppélia* and *The Nutcracker*. Hoffman worked as a lawyer and wrote at night using a pen name. But he was found out and punished when he parodied his co-workers in one of his novels.

Almost fifty years after Hoffman's death, his story "The Sandman" became the inspiration for *Coppélia*. The ballet's music was written by French composer Léo Delibes and choreographed by another Frenchman, Arthur Saint-Léon. Before the ballet had its premier at the Paris Opera on 25 May 1870, there were some problems in casting the lead role of Swanilda. Léontine Beaugrand was chosen by the ballet's producers to dance the part, but she was rejected by the directors of the ballet, who preferred the more famous ballerina Adèle Grantsova. However, Grantsova had to return to Russia and her place was taken by fifteen-year-old Giuseppina Bozzacchi, an Italian ballerina. She danced beautifully and the ballet opened to rave reviews. Tragically, Bozzacchi died of smallpox soon after the opening, and Léontine Beaugrand finally got to dance the part of Swanilda.

In the original production of *Coppélia*, a woman danced the male lead, the reluctant lover, Franz. This casting made it impossible for Franz and Swanilda to perform an elaborate *pas de deux* like the one that is danced today by the couple at the ballet's conclusion. Soon after *Coppélia* was first performed, the original third act was dropped entirely. This meant that the ballet was shorter, with just two acts, which made it perfect for young children. Later the great American choreographer George Balanchine created a new version of the final act, with a magnificent wedding scene.

On 8 November 1884, a one-act version of *Coppélia* staged by A. Bertrand opened at the Empire Theatre in London — thirty-six years before a full-length production was staged there. In 1887 the ballet was produced in America and in 1910 the famous Russian ballerina Anna Pavlova made her U.S. debut in the role.

Coppélia

The Girl with the Enamel Eyes

ONCE, IN A TOWN IN OLD GALICIA, there dwelt a mysterious old man named Dr Coppélius, who lived in a small, dark house on the city square. In all the windows and around the balcony on the first floor, deep green curtains were drawn tight against summer or winter, sunshine or rain. It was as if the house and Dr Coppélius himself were allergic to daylight.

The people in the town gossiped about the old man all the time. They said he was a magician, a sorcerer, an alchemist. But no one actually knew what he did. What they said was simply rumors, guesses, lies.

Now one day, Dr Coppélius limped out of his house, walking unsteadily with the aid of a cane. Anyone watching might have supposed a great sorcerer like Coppélius could keep himself from aging, but in fact the old man was painfully bent over. Reaching the center of the square, he turned and looked up at the balcony of his house. There, the curtains were drawn back to reveal a lovely girl with long blonde braids sitting in a chair, reading. This was the first time she'd ever shown herself. Indeed, this was the first time the deep green curtains had ever been opened.

"Coppélia!" he cried out. "My lovely daughter!" He waved. Wrapped up in her book, Coppélia seemed not to notice him.

Strangely, Dr Coppélius was not concerned by her lack of response. He just rubbed his hands together, as if well satisfied, then went back into the dark house.

But someone else had noticed the girl on the balcony and heard the old man calling to her. That someone was Swanilda, a beautiful village girl with long, dark hair. She was glowing with happiness because Franz, her young man, had just asked her to marry him. So great was her joy, she wanted to share it with everyone she met, and so she waved to Coppélia on the balcony. But Coppélia never looked up from her book.

Swanilda tried again, and still there was no reaction. "Snob!" she exclaimed and turned away. Just then she noticed Franz coming up the street. She was about to run to him when she saw that he, too, was waving. But not at her — at Coppélia, sitting so still, lost in her book.

Furious, jealous, stunned, Swanilda shook her fist at the reading girl. Then she hid behind a fence to see what would happen next. Franz waved at the girl again and then — gasp! — blew her a kiss. At this, Coppélia finally put down her book, looked up and waved back.

Swanilda's heart fluttered, stuttered, almost stopped. Is this a new flirtation, she wondered in despair. Or has Franz been false all the time?

All at once, old Coppélius appeared by the window leading on to the balcony. As if upset by Franz's attentions to Coppélia, he drew the dark curtains tight shut, hiding his lovely blonde daughter from view.

Weeping, Swanilda ran off toward her own house, certain now that Franz no longer loved her. Heartbroken, she suddenly noticed a butterfly alight on the ground before her. A butterfly! It seemed some sort of omen. Franz was like a butterfly, all right, flitting to all the bright flowers. He could never resist a pretty face. Swanilda carefully picked up the fragile creature, turned, and ran back up the street toward Dr Coppélius's house.

Franz was still standing below the balcony, gazing up as if transfixed. Hearing footsteps, he looked around and saw Swanilda coming toward him. Quickly pasting a smile of welcome across his face, he turned to her.

Maybe he still loves me, thought Swanilda. She reached out to him, but all he did was take the butterfly from her outstretched hands and pin it to his shirt. Such a cruel gesture, thought Swanilda. He doesn't love me at all!

"How could you act this way!" she cried.

"What way?" Franz asked, sounding puzzled.

"To flirt with another just after we made our pledge…"

"But I never…"

"You did! I saw you!"

"But Swanilda!" Franz cried. "I love only you."

She broke into weeping. "I saw how much you love me!"

Suddenly, the square, which moments before had been empty of people, filled with all their friends. The young men thumped Franz on the back, the young women kissed Swanilda on the cheeks. "Congratulations! Congratulations!" they cried. "When is the wedding day?"

Franz grinned and tried to hold Swanilda close, but she pulled away. "There is no wedding day," she said.

Her friends thought that a date had not yet been set and their noisy celebrations continued.

"I love you, not her," Franz whispered to Swanilda.

She thought about him waving and blowing a kiss to the girl on the balcony, and what she heard him say was: I love you not.

Just then the burgomaster — the mayor of the town — came into the square. An important-looking man, with an important-looking belly, he held up his hands. "Friends, citizens …" he tried to quiet them. "Children!" he cried, hoping to get their attention. At last they listened. "Tomorrow we are to receive a great gift from the lord of the manor — a new bell for our clock tower. And a celebration to go with it!"

A real celebration! The square buzzed with excitement. Tomorrow!

The burgomaster held up his hands again — meaty hands, with fingers like sausages. "To go along with the celebration," he cried, "his lordship has announced that he will give handsome dowries — bags of gold — to any girls who are married tomorrow."

At this, all the girls gazed longingly at their sweethearts, but Swanilda would not catch Franz's eye. Even when the burgomaster gave her an ear of wheat to shake, and so hear true love's message, all she heard was: I love you not. Throwing the wheat to the ground, Swanilda told her horrified friends, "We are no longer engaged. He loves that snob, Coppélia, the sorcerer's daughter."

"Dr Coppélius has a daughter?" asked one girl in surprise.

8

"Who would have thought such a bent old stick could have a child!" exclaimed another.

"And Franz is in love with her, not me," Swanilda told them.

"How can you say such a thing?" asked Franz. "I've never even spoken to her." But his words lacked conviction.

Night fell, like a dark curtain across the square, and the street suddenly emptied. As empty — Swanilda thought — as my own heart. Twisting a finger through her long hair, she went home alone.

Now as it grew dark, Dr Coppélius left his house again, this time looking about nervously, as if afraid to leave his daughter by herself. He locked his front door, making a great show of it, turning the heavy key three times in the lock. Behind him, the lamplighter had just finished lighting the last of the street lamps and the shadows they cast on the cobblestones danced about like revelers at a party.

Just as Dr Coppélius was about to drop the key into his pocket, a band of real revelers came by. They had begun the bell celebration early and, circling round the old man, they tried to induce him to join them.

"Leave me be!" he shouted, shaking his fist at them. He pulled himself away and the key dropped, unnoticed, to the ground, just another shadow on the street.

Not ten minutes later, wanting to cheer her up, some of Swanilda's friends came by with Swanilda, about to take her to dinner. As they walked along the street, Swanilda stepped on the key. Bending down, she picked up the key, and knew at once who it must belong to.

So did her friends.

"Dr Coppélius's house…" whispered one. "The Magic Master!"

"Dare you?" asked another.

"Will you?" added a third.

Swanilda guessed what they really meant. Would she go into the house and confront Coppélius's snobbish daughter, Coppélia?

"Only if you all come with me," she replied.

The girls nodded one at a time. Secretly, they had each wanted to see inside the sorcerer's house anyway. So, hand in hand in hand, they crept up to the front door. Swanilda put the key in the lock. One …two … three times it turned. Then the lock snapped open. The door creaked as she pushed against it. And … they were in.

Now, no sooner had the girls entered the dark living room, than Franz came into the square carrying a ladder. If Swanilda no longer loves me, he told himself, I shall plead my case to the beautiful Coppélia. Franz was in love with being in love.

He settled the top of the ladder against the balcony and started to climb up.

Just then, back into the square hobbled old Coppélius. Having discovered the key was missing from his pocket, he was hurrying home. But what was this — a ladder, leaning against his house? Angrily, he shook it until Franz fell off. Then he hit the poor lovesick boy with his cane until Franz had to run off to avoid being beaten to death.

Mumbling to himself, the old man went to his front door. To his horror, he found it standing wide open. In he went into the living room, his cane raised in front of him.

Meanwhile, Franz crept back to the square and, seeing the coast was clear, set the top of the ladder once more against the balcony and started up again.

But what of the group of girls led by Swanilda? When they'd first entered the darkened living room, they had lit a candle, which threw a flickering light around the room.

"Who is this?" Swanilda exclaimed, startled to find the room filled with people. The girls bunched together to stare at the figures around them. Some were sitting, some standing, some bent over, hands nearly touching the floor.

"Out! We must get out!" cried one girl. Another started whimpering and a third burst into tears.

"Be quiet!" Swanilda commanded. "Look at them." She pointed to one after another of the figures around them.

"I don't want to look," said the whimperer, her hands covering her face.

"None of us do," echoed the other girls.

"But see, they are not moving. Not moving and not breathing." Swanilda put her

hands on her hips and laughed out loud. "They are just dolls," she said to her friends. "The old man plays with life-sized dolls!"

Indeed, they were just dolls. But what odd characters. A Chinese gentleman in golden robes was perched on a stool. A clown in patches stood bent over from the waist. A knight in shining armor held his sword raised above his head. And there were others, too, all in different costumes and poses. The girls went from one to another, no longer afraid.

Then Swanilda found the curtain that closed off the balcony. Opening it slightly, she discovered the most astonishing thing of all. Sitting in a wheeled chair behind the curtain, book in hand, was Coppélia, the old man's snobbish daughter, her blonde hair slightly askew.

Daughter! She, too, was a doll! Franz is in love with a doll! Swanilda giggled to herself.

Just then, one of the girls accidentally collided with the Chinese gentleman and he began to move, nodding his head and throwing out his hands. The girls giggled.

"*Moving* dolls!" Swanilda suddenly remembered Coppélia waving at Franz.

The girls repeated it to one another: "Moving dolls!"

"Let them all move then," commanded Swanilda.

One by one, the dolls were set in motion, though none of the girls could figure out how to start Coppélia. Beautiful and still, she waited serenely in her balcony chair.

All of a sudden, there was a loud cry and in came the old man, his cane held high. "Vandals!" he cried. "Intruders!"

Swanilda quickly blew out the candle and Dr Coppélius swung his cane around in the dark. This was too much for the girls and they ran screaming from the house. All, that is, except Swanilda. Instead of running away, she ducked behind the curtain and hid on the balcony until all her friends had gone.

At last, the old man calmed down and lit one of his lamps. As he walked about looking at his dolls, he spoke aloud with increasing worry. "They have touched my people. They know. *They know!* But have they touched my daughter? My Coppélia? What a turn. What a turn!" He pulled aside the curtain and walked on to the balcony just as Franz stepped in off the ladder. Grabbing the boy by the ear, he shouted, "You, again!"

"Please, sir, please," Franz said. "I love your daughter. Her still beauty has touched my heart. Please, sir, I want to speak to her."

"Speak to her? Ha! What you ask is impossible," said Dr Coppélius.

"But if I do not, I will die!" Franz cried, hand over his heart. He had not felt that passion a moment before, but now he was certain of it.

"Nonsense," Coppélius said. "Boys do not die of love. Come, have a drink and we will talk about this." Slowly he drew Franz into the living room.

Franz sat down and looked around at the strange figures. He was so fascinated by them that he did not watch as old Coppélius poured an amber-colored liquid into a tumbler and then emptied some powder into it.

Dr Coppélius brought the drink over and handed it to Franz. "Come, my young friend, drink up and let us talk about my daughter, Coppélia."

Thinking the old man was at last warming to him, Franz took a deep draught of the liquid. "Aaaaah," he said, for it tasted of apricots and golden grapes and summer. He took another. Sunlight and the wave of barley in a warm wind. Soon Franz grew sleepy. The magical potion had done its work. His eyes closed. He fell fast asleep in the chair, so still in his slumber, he almost looked like one of the old man's dolls.

"Well, well," muttered Coppélius. An old idea had come to him, one that he'd never had a chance to try out before. But now this meddlesome boy presented the perfect opportunity. He would take Franz's life force and transfer it to Coppélia. Then she would be his daughter in truth. Rubbing his hands with glee, the old sorcerer went to an ancient cupboard in the corner and unlocked it, taking out a heavy leather-bound book of magic spells.

Opening the book, Dr Coppélius read avidly for a few minutes, before marking the page with a dark blue ribbon. Then he went over to the balcony and drew the curtain aside. Coppélia sat, still as always, her book in one hand.

"Soon, my little darling," the old man whispered, "soon you will have real life!" He wheeled her out into the room then went back to his magic book to read it further. "Yes, yes, I think I have it now." Then he walked over to Franz and raised his hands over the sleeping boy, appearing to draw out the life force as if with an invisible magnet. Cupping the life force carefully in his hands, he hobbled over to Coppélia and released it over her.

To his astonishment and delight, Coppélia suddenly tossed the book to one side, then moved her head and arms in a mechanical fashion. Standing slowly, she began to walk stiff-legged around the room.

"My daughter! My daughter!" Coppélius cried, clapping his hands as Coppélia stiffly poked through drawers and opened cupboards. Then she crossed over to Franz and stood over him. Picking up the cup, she raised it to her lips.

"No! No!" cried Coppélius, striking it from her hand. "What are you doing, child? Why are you acting like this?" He watched aghast as his beloved daughter began to race around the room faster and faster. Throwing pictures from the wall, tossing aside scarves and ornaments, she finally kicked the old man's magic book to the floor.

"Stop it, Coppélia, stop it!" Coppélius cried. Grabbing her by the shoulders, he forced her to sit again in her chair.

Just then Franz woke up, his head muddled. Clearly the spell had not actually worked. He moaned and the old man turned on him. "Get out!" Coppélius cried. "Get out!"

Eager to escape from that madhouse, Franz headed to the balcony and climbed back down the ladder at top speed.

In a frenzy, Coppélia jumped up, raced around the room, knocking over all the other dolls, then dashed out of the front door.

"What have I done?" cried the old man. He stumbled out to the balcony to catch a glimpse of Coppélia in the square and what did he find there but the body of a naked, wigless doll lying on the floor. "Coppélia!" he cried, clasping her in his arms, suddenly realizing he had been horribly tricked. For it wasn't Coppélia in the square below but Swanilda, dressed in the doll's costume and wearing her blonde wig, running after the fleeing Franz.

The next day dawned with pearly skies. The new bell was hoisted up into the tower and beneath it stood the maidens who were to be married, along with their husbands-to-be. In that group stood Franz, hand in hand with Swanilda, for he now knew it had been she who had rescued him from the wicked Coppélius. From now on she'd be all things to him — beloved, wife and heroine as well.

Just as the fat-bellied burgomaster was ready to pronounce all the couples man and wife, old Coppélius stomped on to the scene. "Who will pay for the damage to my house, to my people?" he cried, waving his cane about.

There was an awful silence. Then Swanilda stepped forward and bowed her head. In her hand was the bag of gold she'd just received as her dowry. "Here, sir, take this.

All that happened to you was my fault."

But the burgomaster stopped her. "No, my dear, the lord of the manor has sent this extra bag of gold for the old man. All debts have been paid in full. Now let us celebrate."

Dr Coppélius left the newlyweds to their drinking and dancing. He wanted no part in their happiness. But high above, from her balcony where the curtains had been opened wide, the doll Coppélia sat watching the celebrations. For once, her book rested, unread, in her lap. And, if you looked very closely, you could see a serene smile on her face as she gazed down at them all.

Swan Lake

INTRODUCTION

Swan Lake opened at the Moscow Imperial Bolshoi Theatre in Russia on 4 March 1877 and was not a success. This came as a great disappointment to its composer, Peter Ilyich Tchaikovsky. Tchaikovsky was a ballet fan and had been very excited when he was asked to write the music for this, his first ballet, which was to be based on popular European folklore of maidens transformed into birds.

As was the custom, the choreographer J. W. Reisinger began his work before Tchaikovsky had even finished writing the musical score. Ballets at the time were not conceived as a whole, but rather pieced together — music, dance and scenery. But this score was written as a complete piece of music, like a symphony. In fact, at its opening, critics did admire *Swan Lake* for its music. Unfortunately, it was then changed by the dancer playing Odette, Pauline Karpakova, who did not like some sections of the score. She replaced these with dances — music and all — from ballets she had performed previously. By the time the production closed, *Swan Lake* had become quite a patchwork of a ballet — and a failure.

Luckily, Tchaikovsky was not deterred from composing ballet music. With French choreographer Marius Petipa, Tchaikovsky went on to create two of the most well-received ballets of all times, *The Sleeping Beauty* and *The Nutcracker*. Then, years later, Petipa re-choreographed *Swan Lake*, using Tchaikovsky's original music. Finally — though after Tchaikovsky's death — the ballet became a critical success.

In Petipa's version, Italian ballerina Pierina Legnani danced the dual role of Odette/Odile. Her "specialty" — a succession of thirty-two fast, whipping turns on one leg, called *fouettés* — was choreographed into the ballet by Petipa. Since then, countless ballerinas have performed Legnani's acrobatic feat.

In some productions, the ending has been changed — with the prince defeating the evil magician and living happily ever after with his queen. But the original ending marks *Swan Lake* as one of ballet's most enduring tragedies.

The Russian ballerina Anna Pavlova was the most famous Swan Queen. On her deathbed, or so the story goes, she asked for one thing — her swan costume. Later, in a tribute to her, the ballet orchestra played and the spotlight fell on the empty stage where Pavlova's swan would have danced one last time.

Swan Lake

ONCE UPON A TIME IN OLD RUSSIA, where magic still held sway, there lived a fair princess named Odette. When she was thirteen, both her parents died and so she became queen before she quite understood what this meant.

In this same time and place lived a sorcerer named Von Rothbart, who hated the royal family, believing that only he was clever enough and strong enough to rule the kingdom. He'd rejoiced when the king and queen died. And then he began to plot against the new young queen. Indeed, it seemed as if he hated everyone and everything. But there was one person Von Rothbart did love, his daughter, dark-eyed Odile. And having grown up at his side, trained in his ways, she was as wicked as he.

Now it is hard enough for a queen to rule well when there are evil men about. But a child queen and an evil sorcerer in one kingdom? Odette never had a chance. Von Rothbart worked for a full year trying to find the right combination of magical ingredients that would put an end to the young queen's reign. Many a field mouse, skylark and toad were killed in his experiments. Many a peasant disappeared from his land.

Then at last, the sorcerer found the magical recipe he was seeking, a spell that twisted bird and girl together. With a sweet-tasting potion and a single word wrenched from the dark regions, he transformed Odette and all her handmaidens into swans — beaks and wings and tails — banishing them to a lonely lake at the very edge of the kingdom.

This left the country in the hands of Von Rothbart and his daughter. And bad work they made of it. What had been a lush and fertile place was now practically a desert, for that kind of evil magic draws its power directly from the land.

Now, seven years later, in a bordering kingdom, where the land was still green and growing, the young prince Siegfried was shortly to be crowned king. His father having just died, the prince's advisors were all insisting that Siegfried should marry — and soon. They gathered in a meeting room to tell him so.

This distressed the prince. "I have no wish to marry without love," he said. Since he loved no particular girl at the moment, he hoped this would silence his advisors.

"The kingdom needs a queen," the council told him. "And an heir."

"The kingdom may need them, but I do not," said Siegfried. "At least not yet." He strode out of the room, leaving his advisors in a muddle.

As he stomped off down the corridor, Siegfried heard gales of laughter and music coming from outside the palace. He put a hand to his head. Of course! He'd forgotten that today was his twenty first birthday and that his friends had arranged a great celebration.

Siegfried's temples had begun to throb. After the quarrel with his advisors, the last thing he wanted was a party. All he really wished to do was to go off alone into the woods and breathe deeply of the free air. But he knew his old tutor, Wolfgang, as well as his friends and the local villagers, would be terribly disappointed if he did not come out to greet them.

He glanced out of a window. Down below, the party-goers were already standing about in the gathering dusk. He would have to go out to them and look pleased to see them. It was his duty as a prince — as a king.

Trudging down the long flight of stone steps, Siegfried then made his way across the front courtyard, past the palace guards and through the gates. The moment they saw him, all the revelers cheered heartily, and the village boys threw their hats into the air.

Siegfried had to smile. He loved his people and knew they loved him. A happy king meant a happy kingdom. If only his advisors would give him a little more time …

Just then, his best friend, Benno, stepped forward from the crowd. "Happy birthday, my prince," he said, grinning, his hair glowing red in the last rays of the setting sun. From behind his back, he brought out the villagers' present: a magnificent new crossbow,

the wood oiled and gleaming. "Because we know how you love to hunt," Benno said. "May this bring down whatever you aim at, and may you aim at only what you wish to bring down." Benno adored making speeches.

Once again the crowd cheered as Siegfried put his hand on the bow. "The perfect gift," he said, smiling. "And I will try it out as soon as this party is over. You have made me very … happy." He held the bow above his head and the crowd cried out his name.

Just then, his mother, the dowager queen, stormed out of the palace. Furiously, she came up to him, shaking her finger. "Your father is just dead and you celebrate with friends?" she exclaimed. "Shame on you, Siegfried. Shame!" She took him by the arm and led him back into the palace. "You must think about the good of the kingdom, not such frivolities. Your father did not have parties. He did his work. So must you."

"But Mama," he began, as they strode down the marble hall. However, she was like a river in full spate, a flood that could not be dammed up. "The council tells me you did not listen to them, but you must, Siegfried. Choose a bride. Do it tomorrow." It was not a plea but a command. The only way she knew how to speak to him.

Siegfried's head drooped. He was in despair. He knew his mother was right, but he had no desire to wed.

"Tomorrow," she said again and the word tolled in his ears like a death knell.

He tore himself from her grasp and went out into the palace gardens where he stopped for a moment to watch a flock of snow-white swans sail overhead. How he envied them their freedom.

Benno found him there, looking at the sky. "Let us go hunting, my lord," he suggested. "There is a full moon tonight and the hunt will take your mind off things. Besides, you can try out your new bow."

"If only it were that easy," Siegfried said, but allowed himself to be drawn away.

Before it was completely dark, the prince and his closest companions went off following the route of the swans, going due north. They went through woods and moors, over stone walls and across treacherous bogs. The moon came up, white and cold, and still the hunting party went on, crossing over into the bleak land ruled by Von Rothbart, though they did not know it.

Little grew in the hard, cracked soil, neither flowers, nor ferns, and twisted trees wept their few leaves on to the stunted, brown grass.

"I do not like this place," Benno said.

The others agreed. But Siegfried found that the bleakness of the land echoed his own feelings. "We go on," he said.

After a while, they came to a mysterious lake, its waters dark and peaty, the shoreline clogged with dead reeds.

"I like this even less," said Benno.

"It suits me," Siegfried said. "I expect it suits the swans, too." Though in fact they hadn't seen the swans for some time. "I will stay here a while, but you go that way." He pointed farther north.

"We will stay with you," Benno insisted.

"No. I command you to leave. I want to be alone for a while. Do not worry. I will be fine. And perhaps you can send the swans my way." Siegfried smiled, though Benno was not comforted by it. Still, the prince had ordered them gone and so, with reluctant hearts, the hunting party moved north.

No sooner had the men left, than Prince Siegfried spotted the very swans they'd been speaking of, swimming around a bend of the lake, each long neck gracefully curved. Siegfried was entranced. Hiding himself behind the trunk of a dying tree, he set his bow on the ground. The swans were simply too lovely to shoot.

Moving silently over the dark waters, the swans left scarcely a ripple on the surface of the lake. Above them the moon hung like a brilliant lantern.

Siegfried hardly dared to breathe.

The swans came to the shore, waddled up on to the land and then, one by one, stepped out of their skins. Stepped out of their skins! Siegfried's mouth opened and closed, then opened again. He could not say a word.

Out of each of those feathered skins rose a beautiful maiden dressed all in white, with long legs and supple arms and hair the color of corn shimmering in the moonlight.

Siegfried felt he could not intrude on this most miraculous of moments and stood as still as stone. Then he noticed that one of the maidens shone brighter than the rest, on her head a circlet of gold. Suddenly he could not help himself. He stepped away from the tree and went swiftly to the beautiful maiden. Kneeling, he declared, "Fair maid, I have never seen anyone like you. Pray tell me your name."

She cast her eyes down and said in a gentle voice, "My name is Odette, Queen of the Swans. I am under a terrible enchantment. During the day my handmaidens and I

23

must take to the sky as birds, prey to hunters and great eagles alike. Only at night can we come down to land, regaining our human form for as long as it is dark. This lake is our refuge."

Prince Siegfried reached for her hand. "Is there no way to end this cruel enchantment? Tell me and I will do it, fair one."

She let her hand rest in his for a moment, where it lay, small and warm. "Only if someone who has never loved before swears an undying oath to me, only then can the spell be broken. But should he prove unfaithful, I will be condemned to remain a swan for ever."

Siegfried placed his palm over his heart. "I do so swear, on my honor as a prince, as one soon to be a king. I am yours, fair Odette, Queen of the Swans, now and for ever." Then he gathered up both her hands in his. "Tell me the name of the evil one who has put this spell on you, for I shall kill him myself."

Odette shivered. "No, no — if you do that, my prince, the spell will never be broken, and I shall remain a swan."

Just then, Benno and the other hunters returned. They saw the prince, the lovely girls, the white discarded skins.

"My prince!" Benno shouted, his bow raised, for he did not know what to make of the scene, and did not want his prince mixed up with magic.

Siegfried raised his hand. "Put down your bows. These are merely maidens under an enchantment. What has happened to them is not their fault. We must help them, not hurt them."

The first light of dawn began its slow creep over the hills. The dark lake began to redden. Odette and her maidens cried out, their calls hoarsening. Clad in their feathered skins once more, they sprouted beaks and wings, and — with a great leap into the air — they were gone.

Prince Siegfried and his companions slept a little by the lakeside and then came home later in the day to find that the queen had prepared a great ball for her son. Ambassadors from many countries were waiting to greet Siegfried, the medals on their jackets clinking and clanking as they talked. Clearly this ball had been long in the planning. Siegfried knew his mother never left anything to chance.

"You railed at me for my party," said Siegfried, "and now you throw a ball!"

"This ball is not for fun," she told him briskly. "It is for choosing your bride."

"My bride?" He had forgotten all about that.

"Go and change," she said. "And then come down and be charming. To them."

She pointed to a variety of lovely girls who each came forward, curtsied, then preened before the prince.

But Siegfried hardly noticed them. He went up, changed into a suit of green velvet, pinned his own medals to his jacket and brushed his hair. He did not take time to look in the large mirror that hung on his wardrobe. What did it matter how he looked to the girls waiting below? He already knew whom he would marry: Odette, the swan maiden. Still, obedient as ever to his mother's wishes, he was determined to be thoroughly charming for this one evening. He could afford it. He went back down the stone stairs.

In the garden, musicians were playing their viols and oboes under the shining eye of the moon. The music reminded Siegfried of the swans swimming over dark waters, hardly disturbing the surface. He smiled. He knew that while he was at this silly ball, Odette would be resting with her maidens on the lakeshore. Safe for now.

Entering the ballroom, Siegfried saw it was teeming with people waiting to hear his choice. He nodded at them, at Benno, at his tutor, Wolfgang. Let them wait, he thought.

One by one, the maidens came forward to greet Siegfried, but his mind — and heart — were by the dark lake. He would keep it a secret until the spell had been broken. He would tell his mother only that he had found the one he would marry. She would have to be content with that.

Seeing him smile, the queen came over and put a hand on his shoulder. "Now you are acting the king," she said. "Your father would be proud."

Suddenly there came a loud fanfare and two late guests were announced. "Presenting Count Von Rothbart and his daughter."

Prince Siegfried looked up and was so startled that he shook off his mother's hand. Standing next to the grim-faced gentleman was an astonishingly beautiful girl, the very image of the swan maiden, now dressed in a dark gown.

"Odette!" The single name burst from Siegfried's lips. But how could this be? He'd thought her safe at the lake.

What the prince could not know was that this was not Odette, but Odile who, by her father's dread magic, had been transformed into the dark mirror of Odette.

As if in a dream, Siegfried went over to Odile, bowed, took her hand and led her into the dance. As if enchanted, he drew her close, pressed her to him. "My beautiful Odette," he whispered in her ear, still mistaking her for the girl he loved. And she, as wicked as her father, never told him of his mistake.

The moment he spoke those words, there was a frantic beating at the ballroom windows. A girl, as beautiful and fair as a swan, struck her fists over and over on the glass, trying to catch Siegfried's attention. But it was no use. The prince was caught in Von Rothbart's spell, in the spell of Odile's transfigured beauty. He had eyes only for her, ears only for the music to which they danced.

Seeing the prince so transfixed, the musicians played all the louder, drowning out the frantic sounds of the girl in the garden, beating upon the glass. So Siegfried, all unknowing, danced and danced with the beautiful Odile, while around them the guests could only watch. Astonished, Benno shrugged and Wolfgang chuckled. The queen sat on her throne with a satisfied smile on her face.

At last the music ended and the musicians paused for a moment to select another piece. The girl on the grass took a deep breath and brushed away her tears.

Siegfried stepped back from Odile, though he would not let go of her hand. "Come," he said, his voice thick with enchantment. He led her before her father, the hawk-faced Von Rothbart.

"Sir, I would marry your daughter, Odette."

Von Rothbart smiled, which did not improve his grim looks. Like his daughter, he did not let the prince know of his mistake. All he had hoped for, all he had worked for, was about to come true. But he chose his words carefully. Magic must always be precise. "Will you swear to love this girl, whose hand you hold, for ever?"

"I so swear," Siegfried said, putting his other hand over his heart.

Again, the swan girl ran to the window and beat frantically on the glass. The musicians had not resumed playing and this time Siegfried heard her, turned — and saw her. He looked at the girl whose hand he held and then back again at the glass. For a moment, he was stunned. Stunned, and then sickened as realization dawned. He had been tricked, deceived, betrayed.

"You!" he said, spitting the word at Von Rothbart. He guessed now who the count really was — but it was too late. Too late! The spell had taken hold and his true love, Odette, would be a swan for ever.

28

"Odette!" Siegfried cried, pulling himself away from the false maiden's grasp and racing from the ballroom.

The court was in confusion, the queen appalled, while Von Rothbart and his daughter laughed aloud in triumph.

Broken-hearted, Odette made her way back to the lake, to the clotted reeds, to tell her maidens what had happened. Her face was swollen from weeping.

When they saw her, the maidens jumped to their feet and gathered around her.

"Alas," she said, "I no longer wish to live." She tried to pull away from her friends and leap into the cold water while still in human form, but they held her tight and would not let her go.

"No, madam, no!" they cautioned. "Some good will come of this. Von Rothbart shall not win."

At this, she grew quieter. Hope, like a candle, flickered in her breast.

Meanwhile, desperate to find his way back to the lake, Siegfried ran through the night. North, he told himself, north. Tree branches slapped him in the face, roots tripped him, mud sucked at his feet, but still he ran.

Guessing the prince's intentions, the evil sorcerer uttered three words and twisted his cap around three times. Once for wind, once for rain, once for sleet and hail. The skies turned dark, a howling filled the air, and raindrops as thick and hard as stones began to fall.

But nothing — nothing — could keep Siegfried from his task. He battled through the wild and dreadful storm, drenched and shivering. North, he reminded himself, and north again.

When he reached the dark lake at last, the winds suddenly ceased, the rain and sleet and hail disappeared as quickly as they had started. The full moon was reflected in the still water, a perfect silver circle.

On the shore stood Odette, surrounded by her maidens.

Siegfried flung himself at her feet, begging her forgiveness. "I did not know," he said. "I love only you."

She looked down at him, her eyes deep pools. "My love, you were tricked. There is nothing to forgive."

"Then all will be well?" He stood and embraced her.

29

She shook her head. "No, my prince. Nothing will ever be well again. I shall be a swan for ever."

"Then I will join you!"

She took her hand from his and, before anyone could stop her, she ran away and threw herself into the lake. For a moment, the water made furrows in her skirts, like a scallop shell. Then down and down and down she sank, into the cold depths.

Without a word more, Siegfried ran after her, dived into the lake and disappeared into the dark waters.

On shore, the swan maidens shivered and wept.

But it is said — and believed by those who truly care — that their bodies were found later, lying hand in hand at the bottom of the lake.

Siegfried and Odette were united at last in love.

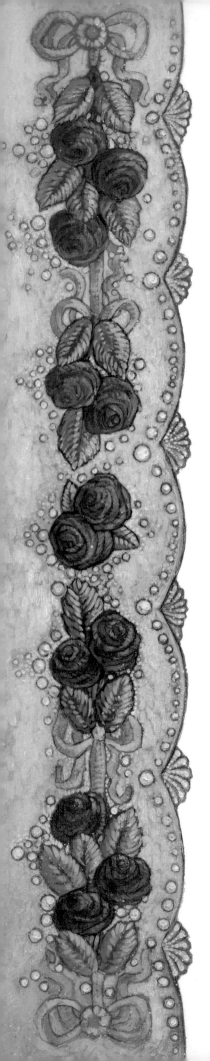

Cinderella
INTRODUCTION

Almost every child knows the story of *Cinderella*: how a young girl is treated as a lowly servant by her evil stepmother but, through a fairy's magic, finds wealth and happiness. It is a tale that has been passed down through the generations in almost every culture. So it should come as no surprise that the story should have been turned into a ballet. Even before the Russian composer Sergei Prokofiev wrote the music for the version of *Cinderella* that is performed today, the ballet had been danced on stages in France, England, America, Russia and practically everywhere in between.

Prokofiev began composing the music for *Cinderella* in the 1940s, but was interrupted by World War II when Germany began bombing Russia. Being a loyal supporter of his country, he turned his attention to writing military marches for the Red Army, and then to composing *War and Peace*, a patriotic opera based on the novel by the great Russian author Leo Tolstoy. But finally, in 1944, Prokofiev was able to return to the composition of *Cinderella*. Another Russian, Rostislav Zakharov, choreographed the ballet, even though certain sections of the music were considered quite difficult to arrange dance steps for, and on 15 November 1945 the ballet opened at the Bolshoi Theatre in Moscow, with Galina Ulanova dancing the title role.

While Prokofiev's score strove to make the characters appear much like real people, many productions preferred to make the stepsisters more exaggerated and comic, using male dancers for the parts. In 1948, Frederick Ashton choreographed Prokofiev's *Cinderella* as the first full-length storybook ballet created in England. It was so popular, it helped turn a small ballet company into what is now the Royal Ballet, one of the top companies in the world. Ashton himself played one of the stepsisters.

In the New York production of the ballet, a new character — a cat — was introduced. This cat gave the ballerina playing Cinderella someone to dance with and he unfastened her shoe, because ballet slippers are tied tightly and it is therefore difficult for a ballerina to "lose" her shoe, as Cinderella must. During one performance of the ballet, not only did Cinderella lose her slipper, but the Prince — danced by Paul Petroff — lost his shoe by accident, which the audience found very funny.

Cinderella

THE LARGE HOUSE SITTING in the middle of a rambling garden was like a stone set in a bronze ring that has gone green with age. It was not worth much now but had once been well loved. Inside the house, the family had settled down for the evening in front of the fire. A quiet evening of warmth and …

"My scarf!"

"MINE!"

Two voices, sharp and edgy, cut across the quiet of the drawing room. Krivlyaka and Zlyuka, as harsh and ugly as their names, were once again quarrelling.

Papa looked up from his newspaper and shook his head. Mama, busy with her sewing, merely shrugged.

Only Cinderella — lovely in the firelight — hoped against hope that her stepsisters' quarrel would quickly be resolved. Otherwise it would spill over, as always, and they would start picking on her.

"My scarf!" Krivlyaka cried.

"MINE!" Zlyuka answered back.

Mama stood up, took the scarf from them and, with a snip of her embroidery scissors, cut it in two. A wail from the sisters went from low to high. "Mama!" they screeched. "How *could* you!" Then they spotted Cinderella.

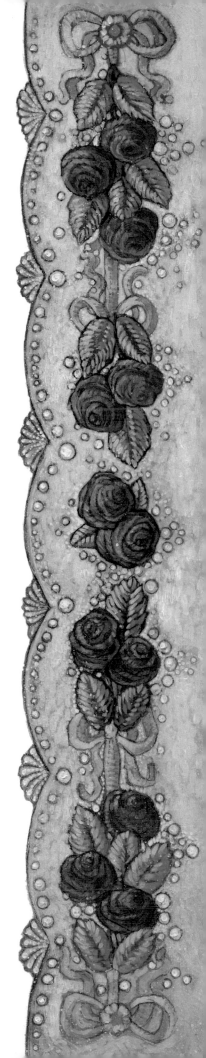

"Her fault anyway," said Zlyuka, throwing down her half of the scarf. And with this Krivlyaka agreed.

Cinderella put her head down and tried to ignore them. She knew they'd eventually get tired of bullying her and go away, as long as she didn't fight back. And after a while, they stopped, as she knew they would. Her stepsisters left her alone at last — her father and stepmother had gone to bed already — and Cinderella set about tidying the room. Dustpan and broom her only partners, she began to dance about in a slow waltz, and dream.

Then, still in a dream, she held the two pieces of scarf up against her shoulder. If only … she thought, but caught herself in time. The mirror over the mantle showed her who she really was. Poor Cinderella, a smudge on her nose, Cinderella the cleaning maid who had once been the only daughter of the house, her father's favorite. Until Stepmother had come with her nasty daughters. She could have wept, but didn't. Weeping — like dreaming — never achieved anything.

The next morning, as usual, Cinderella was busy in the kitchen while everyone else slept in. She had already cleaned the hearth, set the new fire, put the kettle on to boil, and was just sweeping the floor when a loud knock came at the door.

"Cinderella!" It was her stepmother's voice, sharp as a saw's teeth. "Someone is here. Perhaps it is the dressmaker."

Or perhaps it would be the dancing master invited to make her stepsisters ready for tonight's ball at the palace. Or the hairdresser. Or the cobbler. Or …

At least, thought Cinderella, any of these would offer a break in the day's grinding routine. Setting the broom down, she went to the door. Flung it open. Hoped for magic but expected none.

An old woman stood on the doorstep. A crone. Her clothes a dung heap. Her hair a rat's nest. She held out a grimed hand.

Cinderella knew better than to let the old woman in, but … "Here," she whispered, taking a crust of bread from her apron pocket, a crust she'd been planning to eat for her own breakfast. She handed it to the old woman. "It is all I have. May this comfort you, Granny."

The crone nodded. Smiled. There was a moment between them. Not magic exactly, but warmth. Then she was gone.

35

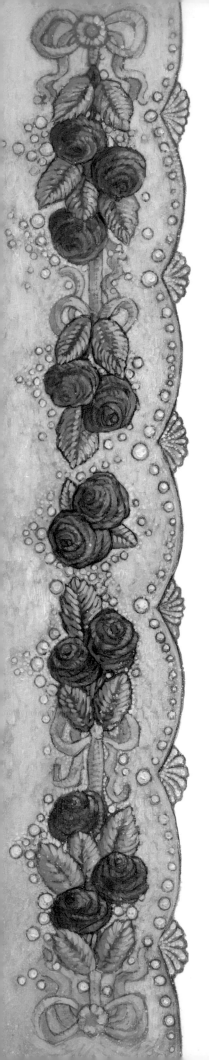

Another knock at the door. This time Cinderella opened it without being asked. It was the dressmaker. Then the hairdresser. Then the dancing master. Then the musicians. She led them into the drawing room.

One by one by one during the long day, the visitors tried to turn the awkward, ugly stepsisters into young ladies graceful enough to catch the prince's eye, for it was thought that he would choose a wife this very night at the ball.

Cinderella watched as they each tried their best with the stepsisters. A hopeless task, she thought. Silk purses out of sows' ears.

The flurry of activity ended as quickly as it had begun, and all the visitors were finally bustled out of the door, closely followed by the family — stepmother, father and stepsisters — on their way to the ball.

Only Cinderella was left behind. Alone. Hand on the broom once again, as if resting her palm lightly on a partner's shoulder, she began to dance. Unlike her stepsisters, she moved with unconscious grace. Her worn skirts — the hem carefully sewn and resewn at the bottom — belled out around her. She was thankful to be alone. Alone, she could pretend.

But she was not alone after all. Someone else was watching. Cinderella looked up, startled, and beheld a pair of eyes that seemed the same as the old crone's but … it was a young woman now standing before her. The old woman might have changed form, but she had not forgotten Cinderella's kindness and the crust of bread.

"A good heart deserves a good evening," she announced and, clapping her hands, she summoned her helpers. Spring arrived carrying a gossamer dress, spun of milkweed and moonlight. Summer brought a spray of wild roses to wind around her hair. Autumn came holding a cloak the color of the last leaves. Winter held up diamonds as bright as icicles to drape around Cinderella's neck and wrists and to twine in her hair.

Stunned into silence, Cinderella could only gawk in wonder as the fairies spun her around and around, helping her into the gossamer dress, the spray of wild roses, the diamonds, the cloak, combing her hair and getting her ready for the ball.

Then the fairy with the old crone's eyes said, "You look lovely, my dear. But something is still missing."

Cinderella looked at herself in the mirror over the mantle. The reflection was not what she expected. Gone was Cinderella in her patched, worn dress. Looking back at her was a princess from some far-off land, breathtaking in roses and diamonds.

"Missing?" She could not guess what could be missing.

The fairy chuckled and snapped her fingers. "Finally, two slippers, crystal and clear, made with love for you, my child." She handed them to Cinderella. "Put them on! Put them on!"

Cinderella did as she was told, then stood quite still, her eyes closed. Was it all a dream? When she opened her eyes again, to her surprise, she was still in the gossamer gown, her hair draped with pink roses and ice jewels, the cloak on her shoulders, the crystal slippers on her feet.

"Now, child," the fairy warned her, "magic comes with rules and you must obey them."

Cinderella curtsied. She would obey any rules, just to be allowed to wear such a dress, such slippers, such jewels.

"Be home by midnight's final chime for, on the stroke of twelve, all your fine clothes will disappear. You will be dressed in rags once more, a servant in your father's house once again."

"Midnight," Cinderella whispered, to show she understood.

Then, with a wave of her wand, the fairy changed a great orange pumpkin from the garden into a coach. With another wave of her wand, six rats became six horses and three mice became the footmen and driver. And away Cinderella sped to the prince's ball.

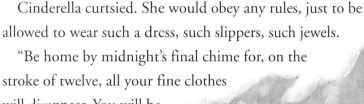

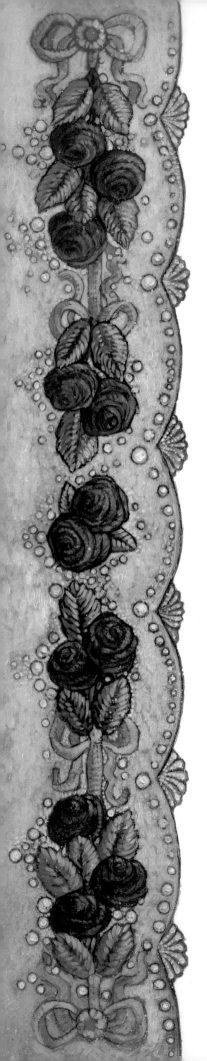

Arriving at the palace, Cinderella was helped down from the coach by the two footmen. They were handsome in their silver-gray livery, but their noses tended to twitch because, underneath all their finery, they were still mice.

The palace was lit with thousands of candles and in the slight breeze it seemed to shimmer. Cinderella could hear music: violins and violas joined in a lively waltz. For a moment she was afraid to go in. But the music set her toes tapping, and the crystal slippers made the sound tink-tink-tink upon the stone stairs. She took a deep breath and started up the steps.

The closer she got, the more the music pulled her in. Soon she was all but running up the stairs. The exertion put roses in her cheeks to match the ones in her hair. Two guards pulled open the heavy wooden doors and she walked in.

The ball was already well under way. Across the great hall couples were whirling and spinning about. Men in colorful coats and women in sparkling dresses looked as lovely as flowers dancing in a garden when a playful breeze blows through.

Gazing around, Cinderella spotted her stepsisters in a far corner, like swine in finery, trying to do the dances they'd been taught. But they hardly knew left foot from right. They bobbed when they should have bowed, hopped where they should have skipped. It would have been laughable if it had not been so sad.

And then the prince entered the ballroom, a young man of regal bearing, his hair tied back with a blue velvet ribbon. Though he was not smiling, still he charmed everyone. Even the stepsisters. Especially them.

But he did not ask any of the women to dance. Instead he sat down on his throne and looked around the hall, as if waiting for magic.

Not every time one waits for magic does it appear. The prince knew this, yet still he waited. For magic. For love.

And then a strange thing happened. A girl who had been standing by the great wooden doors took off her leaf-colored cloak and handed it to a servant. No, not just a girl: a princess. A princess with her hair twined about with roses and wearing diamonds as bright as icicles. A young woman of such grace and bearing, she had to be enchanted.

Or at least the prince was — enchanted. He stood up, walked through the dancers, across the hall and straight over to her. He held out his hand and she gave him hers, a small hand, but surprisingly strong and rather callused. She looked up at him, her eyes

even more sparkling than the diamonds, the roses in her cheeks brighter than the ones
in her hair.

He took her in his arms and they began to dance. And dance. And dance
some more.

She — drab Cinderella an hour before and now a sparkling princess — danced with
the prince as if in a dream. Around them the other guests looked on. Some whispered
behind their fans. Some matched them step for step. Some were jealous, others simply
amazed.

Did Cinderella notice? No more than the prince did. They saw only each another as
they danced.

But enchantments follow rules. Magic has consequences. The clock began to strike
the midnight hour and the gossamer girl looked up from her dream, startled.

"Midnight!" she cried. "I must fly!"

Such was the moment of enchantment, that the prince thought she meant to sprout
wings. To become a lark, a butterfly, a moth. But instead, she pulled herself from his
arms and raced away, like a startled deer, a hare before the fox, leaving only a single
crystal slipper behind.

Early the next morning, as the sun's light was just beginning to creep into the sky,
Cinderella awoke by the hearth fire. Perhaps it had only been a dream, she thought
as she started to doze once again. For how could she have had a gossamer gown,
a spray of wild roses and cascades of ice-bright jewels in her hair? How could she
have gone to the ball and danced with the prince himself?

But something clinked in her pocket as she woke up. When she reached her hand in
to see what had made the sound, she drew out a single crystal slipper.

Not a dream, then, she told herself. Magic!

Standing, she found the broom where she had left it, leaning against the hearth.
"My lord," she whispered, curtsying to it, "I would love to have this dance with you."
Then, holding the broom tenderly in her arms, she began a slow waltz, though the
only music was in her head, in her heart, in her soul.

Just then, her stepsisters, Krivlyaka and Zlyuka, and her stepmother and father came
back from the ball. The sisters lurching on aching feet. Giggling. All but oinking with
pleasure.

39

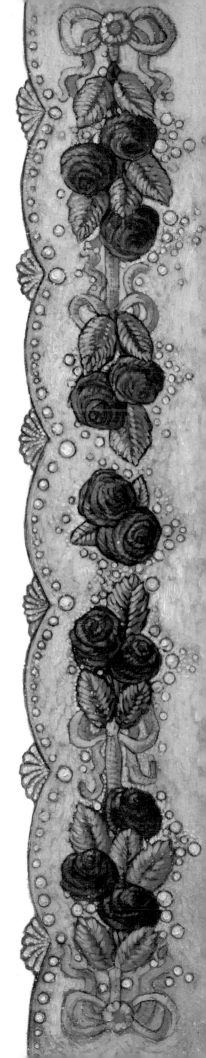

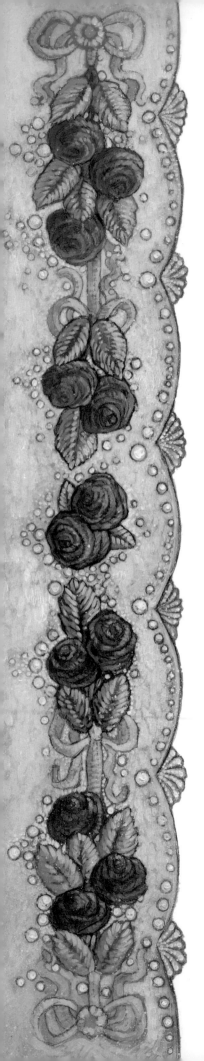

Cinderella's broom companion was set back against the hearth. She was servant, cleaner, maid once more. Midnight had come and gone. The dream was over. The magic had fled, except for what remained in her memory and in her pocket.

But what was that commotion outside?

The prince had come with heralds and a jester — his court advisor — carrying the single crystal slipper.

"I will marry the girl whose foot fits this shoe," the prince had announced.

So, street by street, house by house, the prince and his messengers went, trying the tiny slipper on the feet of big girls and small girls and in-between girls. And now they were at Cinderella's house.

Cinderella opened the door and the prince's messengers held out the crystal dancing slipper. "We must find the girl who fits this," they said. "For she is the one who shall marry the prince."

"My shoe!"

"MINE!"

Two voices, sharp and edgy, cut across the kitchen. Krivlyaka and Zlyuka were quarrelling once again.

"One at a time," their mother warned, raising a finger. "One at a time, my lovelies."

So the messengers tried the dainty crystal slipper on the girls, first on Krivlyaka's foot, then on Zlyuka's. No shoehorn could get it on either foot. Their feet were much too big and as awkward as pigs' trotters.

But who was that lurking near the hearth fire? A serving maid? A tattercoat? A beggar girl come in from the street?

The prince drew near. "Will you try on the shoe?" he asked, for he noticed that her eyes sparkled, and it was not a just trick of the firelight. He saw roses in her cheeks, but the room was not that warm.

"She is no one," cried the stepmother.

"Less than no one," cried the stepsisters.

"I will try," Cinderella whispered, her voice giving nothing away.

She slipped her foot into the crystal shoe.

"It fits!" cried the prince, gently removing the shoe and holding it aloft.

Then Cinderella suddenly — miraculously — drew the matching slipper from her

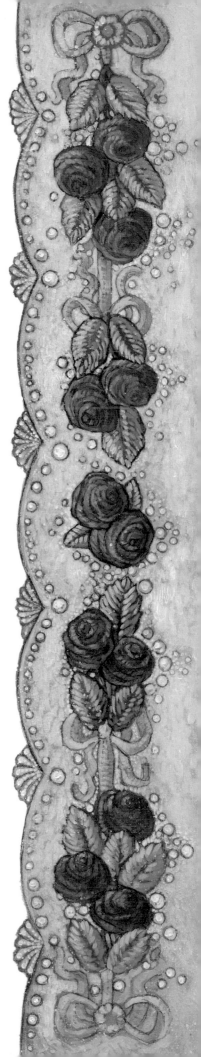

pocket. The prince touched her crystal shoe with his and it rang with a sound as joyous as wedding bells.

"Will you marry me?" he whispered.

"With all my heart," she answered.

The crystal shoes rang out again.

With that, the fairy appeared and, magically, the gossamer dress and the jewels adorned Cinderella once again.

"My prince!" Krivlyaka spat out.

"MINE!" Zlyuka spat back.

But no amount of wrangling would make him theirs. He belonged to Cinderella, of course, not to them.

Cinderella and her prince were married soon after. The fairies danced at their wedding and everyone — except Krivlyaka and Zlyuka, and their mother — lived happily ever after.

The Nutcracker
INTRODUCTION

The Nutcracker is a ballet about the strange, magical events that befall a young girl on Christmas Eve. Like *Coppélia*, it was adapted from one of E. T. A. Hoffman's fantasy tales. Because it is a Christmas story, the ballet is staged during the December holidays by professional companies and dance schools around the world.

All of the different productions have used the same music, written by the great Russian composer Peter Ilyich Tchaikovsky. He was given strict instructions by the choreographer Marius Petipa, who had strong ideas about how the ballet should look, sound and feel. Before Petipa could choreograph the original ballet himself, he became ill and the job fell to his assistant, Lev Ivanov. *The Nutcracker* was completed and opened on 18 December 1892 at the Maryinsky Theatre in St Petersburg, Russia.

The music Tchaikovsky composed may be the only ballet score that is even more popular and recognizable than the ballet itself. "The Dance of the Sugar Plum Fairy" is particularly well known and includes the bell-like tones of an instrument called the celesta, which had never been used in an orchestra before.

After being successfully staged for the first time in Western Europe at the Sadler's Wells Theatre in London on 30 January 1934, *The Nutcracker* continued to grow in popularity. In 1954, American choreographer George Balanchine — who had danced the role of the Nutcracker Prince at age fifteen in Russia — reworked the piece for the New York City Ballet, giving the lead role of Clara to a young dancer. Indeed, *The Nutcracker* is unique among ballets produced today in its use of children in main parts instead of simply as extras on stage. When it was first staged, it was common practice to use a ballet school's younger students in performances as part of their training, but not necessarily as main characters.

In Balanchine's version of the ballet, with a young dancer as Clara, there is no romance between Clara and the prince. But in later productions, notably Rudolph Nureyev's and Mikhail Baryshnikov's, the lead is played by an adult dancer and the romantic *pas de deux* at the palace in the Land of Sweets is danced by Clara and the prince instead of the Sugar Plum Fairy and her cavalier. Whether the main parts are danced by adults or children, *The Nutcracker* never seems to lose its magic, however, and continues to captivate audiences the world over.

The Nutcracker

Christmas Eve at Councillor Stahlbaum's

THE GREAT FIR TREE stood in the front parlor. Beneath its spreading branches, presents lay in their festive wrappings. On every branch shone a candle, and the flames were like the stars over Bethlehem.

A band, hired especially for the occasion, sat in the hallway playing yuletide songs. It was Christmas Eve at Councillor Stahlbaum's. Everyone important in the city would be there to greet the councillor and his family.

"Hurry, Clara!" young Fritz Stahlbaum called, eager to check on the gifts, both the ones with his name attached and the others as well. His sister raced him into the parlor.

They stood together before the giant tree, and Clara thought dreamily: What treasure! Could anything be as wonderful as Christmas?

Just then Grandpapa and Grandmama arrived and, behind them, jumping with excitement, more children with their parents.

"Presents!" the boys cried, and the girls echoed them: "Look at the presents!"

"Come on, I'll show you," said Fritz. He pointed to the gift boxes: short ones with silver paper tied with bright red string, long ones wrapped in pink with gilt ribbons, fat ones and thin ones, and even a round gift that looked as if it might be a globe of the world. The children jostled around and clapped their hands. There were so many presents heaped under the tree.

"When will Papa give out the gifts?" Fritz whispered to Clara.

"When he is ready." She gave him a little smile and he spun away to play with the boys.

Then Councillor Stahlbaum divided the children up. "First a game, then a dance!" he called out.

So there was a game of marching, then a lively dance, and even some of the grown-ups joined in, which made it stuffy — or so Fritz remarked to the boys. Whatever Clara thought about it, she kept to herself.

Before anyone could catch their breath from all that dancing, Councillor Stahlbaum announced: "Time for the presents!"

"Hurrah!" all the children shouted.

There was something for everyone. It was, after all, Christmas Eve at the Stahlbaums'. Soon the room was filled with the sounds of laughter — and of wrapping paper being ripped open.

"A doll!" cried one girl.

"A jeweled box!" cried another.

"Tin soldiers!" cried several of the boys.

Just as the children were settling down to the serious task of playing with their new toys, the door opened. In walked the most extraordinary gentleman any of them had ever seen. Tall, bony and stooped, he was dressed in somber black, with a black patch over one eye, like an ancient pirate.

"Herr Drosselmeyer!" cried Clara, jumping up to greet her godfather. There was always something a bit enchanted about him. She knew that he was an inventor, but suspected, sometimes, that he was much more magical than that.

Drosselmeyer gave her a quick kiss on the cheek, then introduced her to his nephew, a handsome boy just Clara's age.

"I call him my little prince," said Drosselmeyer.

Clara looked at the boy shyly, but she liked him at once. And indeed he was as handsome as a prince. "Welcome to our house," she said.

He grinned at her and, with royal good manners, bowed as well.

Herr Drosselmeyer signaled to a servant to bring in three large boxes, which he opened one by one. To the astonishment of all, they held three life-sized clockwork dolls — Harlequin and Columbine, who soon began to dance together, and then a toy soldier who marched stiff-legged around the room.

47

"More! More!" the boys cried out, while the girls clapped their hands.

But there was only one thing more. From the deep pocket of his greatcoat, Herr Drosselmeyer brought out a final gift.

"For Clara," he said with a flourish. "For my goddaughter."

The present was not even wrapped: a wooden nutcracker in the shape of a soldier with a long nose and a big mouth. Putting a walnut between the soldier's jaws, Herr Drosselmeyer showed Clara how to crack the nut open.

"Oh, Godfather," Clara exclaimed, "this is the most wonderful present I have ever received!" She meant it, too, and cradled the wooden nutcracker in her arms, showing it off to all the girls.

Furious at not being the center of attention, Fritz pushed through the circle of girls. Grabbing the nutcracker from his sister, he held it high above his head. "Now it's mine!" he shouted, then smashed the nutcracker to the floor. "Now it's nobody's!"

The nutcracker broke apart, top and bottom jaws in separate pieces. The big room was suddenly silent.

"Oh, no!" Clara wept. Picking up the pieces, she held them out tearfully to Herr Drosselmeyer.

"Do not worry, child," he said, wiping her eyes with a large handkerchief. Then bandaging the broken nutcracker with the same handkerchief, now wet with Clara's tears, he placed it tenderly in a doll's bed which he set under the tree. The party was over.

Midnight, Christmas Eve

Fritz slept, as naughty boys often do, soundly and untroubled by bad dreams. But Clara tossed and turned in her bed and could not get to sleep. Finally, she got up and tiptoed down the long, winding stairs, in her white nightgown.

She came into the parlor, where the candles on the tree had burned down more than halfway. Looking around, she found the nutcracker where Herr Drosselmeyer had left it, in the doll's bed. Taking it in her arms, she curled up on the sofa and only then fell asleep. She didn't even wake when her mother came by, checking through the house one last time.

"Poor dear," said Mrs Stahlbaum and covered Clara with her shawl. "Christmas will be a brighter day." Then she blew out the lamps but left the candles on the tree ablaze in case Clara should wake and need to find her way back up the stairs.

The shimmering tree cast strange shadows in the room. The clock struck midnight, its loud chimes echoing in the room. Rubbing her eyes, Clara awoke. She sat up and looked about.

What's that? Clara thought she saw something in the shadows — her godfather in his greatcoat fixing the nutcracker with a screwdriver. When had he taken the wooden doll from her arms? It was a puzzle. Herr Drosselmeyer finished whatever work he was doing, set the nutcracker down in the doll's bed, then, without glancing over at Clara, he left the room.

And what was that? Little scurrying figures hurried across the floor. Clara could not make out what they were, or how many. And that? Something odd was happening to the Christmas tree. It began to grow, rising higher and higher until the tin star at its top poked through the ceiling. Clara felt small and big at the same time. She felt as if the world were suddenly filled with magic.

Suddenly there was a noise behind her and Clara turned. She spotted a gigantic mouse, taller than she was, with a golden crown on its head, nestled between its ears. Clara hurried to get away, hiding behind a long curtain at the window. As she watched, a dozen or more huge mice scurried into view.

Clara trembled at the sight of them and the curtain began to shake. No, the heavy curtain was already being shaken by a strange wind that had come blowing through the room, even though the windows were shut tight against the cold. An eerie and mysterious light filled the room.

Then the toy soldiers under the tree began to stand up one at a time, magically coming to life. Most astonishing of all, the nutcracker was alive as well, sitting up in his little doll's bed and looking around, his long nose twitching, his black eyes bright.

"How curious," Clara whispered to herself, suddenly calm again, as though the nutcracker's presence had given her courage.

All of a sudden, the mice gathered themselves together under the leadership of the fierce Mouse King.

"Charge!" they yelled and rushed at the toy soldiers.

Nutcracker leaped up from the bed. "Soldiers — to me! To me!" he cried.

The tin soldiers gathered quickly by his side and drew their toy swords. Fighting valiantly, they tried to stem the onrush of the mice but — outnumbered and outweighed — they slowly but surely were defeated.

Soon only Nutcracker was left standing, fighting the Mouse King himself with quick thrusts of his sword. But the Mouse King was faster, heavier, meaner. He cornered Nutcracker and rubbed his paws together with gleeful malice; poised to move in for the kill.

Oh, no, Clara thought. I have to do something. But she had no sword, no gun, no weapon. Then suddenly she remembered what Cook did whenever she saw a mouse. Bending over, Clara took off her slipper and, standing up again, took careful aim and threw it at the Mouse King's back.

The slipper hit the Mouse King with a dull thud. He turned to see what had smacked him and, as he did, Nutcracker dealt him a mortal blow. The Mouse King fell to the ground and expired, his whiskers twitching.

With their leader gone, the rest of the mice fled, squealing, back to their hidey-holes.

Clara hurried over to where Nutcracker stood, bent over from exhaustion. When he stood up and turned around to thank her — what a surprise! Gone was the strange nutcracker head with its long nose and big mouth. Instead there was a handsome prince smiling at her, the very image of Herr Drosselmeyer's nephew!

He bowed. "You have saved us all, fair one," he said. Then holding out the Mouse King's crown, he added, "Come with me to the Land of Sweets where we will be well rewarded."

Clara placed the crown upon her head and followed him, a slipper on one foot, the other foot bare, out through the trees and the dancing snowflakes. She never even felt the cold.

In the Land of Sweets

The news of the Mouse King's defeat had already spread. The Christmas tree had told the dried grass outside Councillor Stahlbaum's house, and the blades of grass — being great gossips — had told the reeds by the river's edge. And the reeds, never known for their silence, had whispered the story to the little whitecaps in the river.

All the fairies gathered by the chocolate river heard what had happened, but they could scarcely credit it. After all, the Mouse King and his soldiers had plagued them for as long as they could remember. Led by the lovely Sugar Plum Fairy, they chattered nervously. "Is it true? Can it be real?"

"We will know everything soon enough," the Sugar Plum Fairy told them, holding up her hand for silence. "For soon the prince and Clara will arrive. I have sent our walnutshell boat for them."

"Will they be fierce?" the fairies asked.

"Of course they will be fierce," the Sugar Plum Fairy said. "After all, they have slain the dreaded Mouse King."

Then someone called out, "The boat!" and they hurried to greet it.

The little walnutshell boat rowed itself right up to the shore where pebbles as colorful as boiled sweets were strewn about. The prince got out first and then lifted Clara ashore so that her one slipper would not get wet.

"Not fierce at all," the fairies remarked to one another, both relieved and delighted.

"Welcome to our kingdom," said the Sugar Plum Fairy, bowing low to Clara and the prince. "We have heard the news that has come down the river. But we want to hear the story of what happened directly from you."

The prince smiled and bowed back. Then he told the story — about the nutcracker, the mice, the tall tree, and how Clara had saved him by throwing her slipper at the Mouse King.

"How brave!" the fairies exclaimed, sounding even more delighted. They spun about and clapped and looked a little tipsy with the excitement.

Clara stood by the riverbank, blushing with pleasure, her cheeks as bright as cherry candies.

Then the Sugar Plum Fairy led Clara and the prince to a beautiful palace and into the great hall where a tall table was piled high with sweets. Across the room was a golden throne encrusted with jewels.

"Sit here, eat what you will, and let us entertain you," she told them. "It is to show our thanks to you for having destroyed the terrible Mouse King, who delighted in gobbling up all our sweets."

So Clara and the prince climbed up to the tall throne, and Clara realized that the jewels were not jewels at all but brightly colored candied fruit. She waited until the prince found her a cup of tea, that was both sweet and warming. Then the fairies all began to dance. Hot Chocolate and Coffee and Tea spun about together, then came Candy Canes and Marzipan and even Mother Ginger — with her wide skirts under which little Punchinellos lurked.

After the sweets had finished dancing, the flowers themselves were drawn into a waltz, their petals brightly whirling about until all the colors blurred together.

Clara yawned. It had been a long, tiring night. She ate another chocolate and licked her fingers, just as the Sugar Plum Fairy danced a beautiful *pas de deux* with her cavalier.

Clapping her hands, Clara turned to the young prince. "It is like a dream," she said, "only better."

"Much better," he agreed.

Clara yawned again, her hand over her mouth.

Then the Sugar Plum Fairy came over and took both Clara and the prince by the hand. "Time to go home," she said, leading them out of the hall.

In front of the palace stood a bright red sleigh heaped high with soft blankets and pillows. Hitched to the sleigh were a dozen reindeer, all snorting and eager to be away.

The prince helped Clara in, tucking a blanket around her. Then he settled in himself.

"Goodbye, goodbye, goodbye!" cried the flowers and sweets, Mother Ginger and the Sugar Plum Fairy.

"Good …" Clara began as the sleigh rose into the air. But before she could even finish the word, the movement of the sleigh had rocked her fast asleep.

And when she awoke, was it on the sofa in the parlor of her own home, the little nutcracker clutched safely in her arms? That is how the story ends — if you think it was all a dream. But Clara didn't believe that, nor did the prince. And certainly the fairies from the Land of Sweets knew better.

The Sleeping Beauty
INTRODUCTION

Over a hundred years ago, in the 1890s, a small, shy girl sat spellbound in the audience at the Maryinsky Theatre in St Petersburg, Russia. Watching *The Sleeping Beauty*, she vowed that she would some day dance the part of Princess Aurora herself. That little girl grew up to be the most famous ballerina of all time — Anna Pavlova.

During the nineteenth century, instead of writing ballet music from start to finish, a ballet composer would piece together sections of music that he (or others) had written earlier. But *The Sleeping Beauty* was to be different. The position of ballet composer had just been abolished, and so when choreographer Marius Petipa was commissioned to create a new ballet based on Charles Perrault's fairy tale "La Belle au Bois Dormant" ("Beauty in the Sleeping Wood"), the already renowned composer Peter Ilyich Tchaikovsky was approached to write the complete musical score. It was his second ballet — he had already composed the music for *Swan Lake* — but his first with Petipa.

Petipa liked to work closely with everyone involved in the production. He even used wooden figures to see which groupings of dancers would look the best to the audience. As he would for *The Nutcracker*, Petipa gave Tchaikovsky very strict instructions about how the music should sound and how long each section should last. Luckily, Tchaikovsky was not insulted by this and took direction well. The result was what some critics consider to be the best-rounded ballet ever created.

The central theme of *The Sleeping Beauty* is Princess Aurora's coming of age. This is illustrated in the ballet through three adagios (dances in slow time) — the first when she is a young girl, the second as she falls in love with the prince and the third on her wedding day. Another highlighted dance is that of the Bluebird at the wedding celebration, which is often performed by the same man who dances the role of the evil fairy Carabosse.

The Sleeping Beauty opened at the Maryinsky Theatre on 15 January 1890 with Petipa's daughter Marie dancing the role of the Lilac Fairy. It wasn't until 1916, however, that Anna Pavlova — the shy little girl who vowed some day to dance the part — finally took to the stage as Princess Aurora in a special forty-eight minute version of *The Sleeping Beauty* at the Hippodrome Theater in New York. It was a triumph.

The Sleeping Beauty

ONCE UPON A TIME, when fairies still bestowed both wishes and curses, a certain King Florestan ruled a green and lovely land. Spring and summer were long and gentle, autumn was a riot of color, and winter laid a cool hand upon all. For many years the kingdom was a happy place and the king a monarch who loved to do good.

Now Florestan and his queen had almost everything they wanted or needed, except for a child of their own. Year after year went by and they had all but given up hope, when the queen gave birth to a baby girl. They named her Aurora, which means Dawn, for indeed a new day had dawned in their lives.

As was the custom of the kingdom, the king sent out invitations to all of the fairies to attend Aurora's christening. Led by the beautiful Lilac, the fairies came in a whisper of wings and shimmering in gossamer party gowns to dance around the baby's cradle. Then they gave baby Aurora her christening gifts.

"I will give you generosity of soul," said one, touching the baby with her hand.

"And I add a contented spirit," said the next.

The Fairy of Bravery kissed the baby on the forehead. "You shall be self-assured and very courageous."

Then followed three more fairies who gave Aurora the gifts of truth-telling, beauty of face and voice, and lightness of heart.

At last Lilac came forward, in her gown of palest purple, trailing lilac blooms. She was just bending over the cradle, when — with a crash — the wicked Carabosse entered the room, attended by a host of imps and giant rats. More witch than fairy, more darkness than light, Carabosse swept along the floor in her long black gown and cloak. She stomped across the great hall and shoved her hideous face into baby Aurora's.

"Pah!" she exclaimed, and spittle splattered the baby's blanket. Then the witch turned. Raising her right hand, she pointed at the king and queen. "Why was I not sent an invitation to this child's christening?"

The rats and imps snickered and repeated the question.

Why indeed? The king and queen trembled. They turned to ask the vizier, Cattalabutte, who looked aghast. There was no right answer. Silence seemed best.

But nothing said or unsaid would turn the wicked Carabosse from her anger. "You did not think of me, but I — I have given much thought to you. And to your little baby. So here is *my* blessing. This little bit of sunlight, this Aurora, shall soon fade. When she reaches her sixteenth birthday, she shall prick her finger on a spindle and fall down dead. Hah!"

"Hahahahahaha!" chorused the rats and imps.

The king and queen and vizier recoiled in horror. The fairies were in such a state, their wings beat as fast as a hummingbird's in flight. One by one and two by two, they begged Carabosse to change her mind, but the old witch would not — or could not — undo what she had just done.

At last, Lilac came forward, her mouth set in a thin line. "Wait! I have not yet given my blessing to the child. And while I cannot lift the curse entirely, I *can* soften it."

The room was hushed, waiting.

Lilac continued. "When Aurora is sixteen, she *shall* prick her finger on a spindle and fall down. That is beyond my changing. But she will not be dead. No. She will fall into a long sleep that can only be lifted by the kiss of a handsome prince."

"A long sleep…" the whisper sped around the room.

Carabosse growled at Lilac, like a wild animal at its tamer. She made a wicked, angry sign, and her imps and rats chittered. But Lilac only smiled. This made the old witch even more furious.

"Begone, Carabosse!" cried Lilac, raising a hand. "Trouble this kingdom no more. And take your familiars with you!"

The Lilac Fairy's magic was powerful enough that Carabosse was forced to flee, wrapping her long black cloak around her. The rats and imps darted after her.

After the christening, the vizier, Cattalabutte, advised King Florestan to send a decree throughout the land banning all spindles.

"But how will that help?" the queen asked.

"Think, my dear," Florestan told her. "If there are no spindles anywhere in the kingdom, Aurora cannot possibly prick her finger, can she?"

His wife shook her head. "If that were all that was necessary, we wouldn't need fairy magic." She knew that no comfort is to be had where curses are concerned.

But her husband and the vizier put their faith in decrees of this sort. Indeed, the kingdom ran on such things. And for a long while their plan worked.

Over the next fifteen years, Aurora grew into all the good wishes the fairies had given her. She was brave and spirited, she had a contented soul full of laughter. She was generous and truthful and her voice was as beautiful as her face. Everyone in the kingdom loved her and, after a while, everyone forgot all about the terrible curse.

Everyone, that is, except Cattalabutte, who one autumn day found some women gossiping and knitting together.

Now, knitting needles are not spindles, but they both can prick a finger. Cattalabutte had the culprits arrested at once and was about to send them to jail, when the king and queen pardoned the women.

"No harm done," said the king, who truly loved his people.

"No harm done," agreed the queen, who loved them equally well.

But the knitting needles were taken away nonetheless, as were needles of every shape and size.

Time went by. Things that should not have been forgotten were; things that should have been remembered were not.

Now, on Aurora's sixteenth birthday, a great party was thrown in her honor. It was the day she was to choose her future husband from among the assembled princes. All the children of all the courtiers were invited to the party, and they came with presents and garlands of flowers. They laughed and sang and danced.

Then, one by one, the eligible princes were introduced to Aurora. She smiled at each of them in turn, for she'd been brought up to be polite. She listened to their vows of love.

Yet she remained unmoved. Perhaps she did not feel old enough to be married. Perhaps she did not like any of the princes enough. Or perhaps, since this was her birthday party, she just wanted to laugh and sing and dance the night away without having to make such hard choices.

As she danced — with one prince and another, with the children, then by herself — she felt full of joy. And that joy illuminated her features as if she'd been lit from within by a bright candle.

Suddenly, Aurora found herself face to face with an old woman clad in a dark woolen cloak that covered her from head to toe. The woman's kindly eyes shone back, reflecting Aurora's happiness.

"What is that?" asked Aurora, venturing close, for in the old lady's hand was a strange, wooden toy with a pointed end which she spun around and around.

"A present for you, my pretty," said the old woman. "A gift from my mother and my grandmother, something that means so much to me that I wanted to pass it on to you for, alas, I have no children of my own."

Aurora took the toy. "I thank you kindly, Granny!" she cried. "And may you, too, have great joy on this day."

"Oh, I will," whispered the old woman.

Then Aurora took the toy and turned it over and over as the old woman had done, and the pointed end pricked her finger.

"Oh!" she cried in surprise. "Oh!" Suddenly feeling faint, she stumbled across the room, then swooned in front of her parents seated on their thrones.

The old woman suddenly flung off her cloak and stood before them in a black satin dress, sparkling with dark stars.

"Carabosse!" the king and the vizier, Cattalabutte, cried together.

"It is indeed I!" cackled the wicked fairy. "You may have forgotten me. But did you think *I* would forget?"

The queen screamed and slumped into her chair in a dead faint. A hush descended over the revelers.

Suddenly, there was a flash of purple fire and the Lilac Fairy appeared. She pointed to Carabosse. "Begone, you old witch, for you have already done your worst."

Carabosse left, but she was laughing all the while.

"How can you help, dear Lilac?" wept the king. "For my child lies dead at my feet."

61

Lilac shook her head. "Your memories are truly faulty, my king. Remember — I told you the princess would not die, but merely fall asleep."

"But what good is a sleeping princess to the kingdom?" asked Cattalabutte, quite sensibly. Then, suddenly recalling the rest of Lilac's promise, he added, "And where shall we find a prince to kiss her?" He looked toward the four princes who had already vowed to love Aurora.

But the Lilac Fairy knew that none of those princes was brave or strong or smart or sensitive enough for Aurora. So she did what any good fairy would do. She put the entire kingdom to sleep with a wave of her wand, for would it not have been a real tragedy if Aurora had outslept them all?

The king slept, with the queen in his arms. The boys and girls slept. The four princes slept, as did all the other guests. The cooks and courtiers, the guards and gardeners — they all slept. And as they slept, a great briar hedge grew around King Florestan's castle, a hedge with deadly thorns, to keep the kingdom and its sleeping inhabitants safe from all intruders.

Now, that magical sleep went on for a hundred years. Meanwhile, outside the kingdom there were revolutions and wars, then peace once again and brand new countries rising from the ashes of the old.

In one such country, far to the east of the castle and its briar hedge, lived Prince Florimund, a young man of great energy and wit. He had been out hunting and had arrived back at his father's palace late in the afternoon to discover that a surprise party was in progress. All the courtiers were in the middle of a riotous game of hide-and-seek.

He tried to make his way up to his room without being noticed, but one young woman spotted him and then a second and a third, and soon he was surrounded. But the prince did not desire any of the women there. He simply smiled, shook his head and walked away, from the game, from the party. He would have walked away from the castle if he could.

Suddenly, a beautiful fairy appeared before him as if from nowhere. As it had been years since any fairies had appeared in the world, the prince was understandably surprised. But being a young man who read books, he recognized her at once. The purple gossamer gown and the shimmering wings gave her away. Lilac was as beautiful and changeless as magic allows.

She called the prince to her. "If this party is not to your liking," she said, "I can promise you a grand fairy hunt instead."

A fairy hunt certainly sounded more interesting than his father's surprise party. So Prince Florimund nodded in agreement and followed Lilac down the steps. In the courtyard, for his eyes alone, she summoned up wood nymphs who danced before him.

"But what am I to hunt?" he asked.

She pointed at the nymphs and suddenly, in their midst, appeared an astonishingly lovely girl of about his age. She had hair the color of ripened wheat and eyes as blue as speedwells.

Prince Florimund could not stop staring at her. For the first time, he knew what love was — a pang in the heart that would not go away.

"Who *is* she?" he asked Lilac.

"Your promised bride," she told him. "Princess Aurora. Go to her."

Prince Florimund nodded and chased after the girl, seeking to hold her in his arms. But if this was a hunt, she was too quick for him. She vanished into the shimmering air.

"Aurora!" he cried, but she was gone. So, turning to the fairy, the prince implored, "Bring her back. Please bring her back!"

"She is just a seeming, an apparition," replied Lilac. "I cannot bring her back in the flesh, but I *can* guide you to the castle where she lives, though the way is hard."

Prince Florimund knelt before her. "I will go to her however hard the road. Take me at once."

Lilac smiled, then waved her wand and a boat suddenly appeared, bobbing on the waters of a lovely, winding river that had not been there a moment before. "Step in, my prince."

He stood and, without a moment's hesitation, climbed into the boat. Lilac got in beside him. Then the boat bore them along the river until at last it came to a stop

beside a vast tangled hedge. Beyond the hedge, the prince could see the tops of towers where ancient, tattered banners fluttered in the wind.

"There," said Lilac gesturing to the castle.

"But where is the entrance?" asked the puzzled prince.

"You must make your way through the thorns," said Lilac. "True love awaits you on the other side. Do not be afraid."

"I am not afraid," said the prince. He got out of the boat and went straight up to the briar hedge. There he could see the whitened bones of men who had been there before him, caught in the thorns. Taking out his sword, he raised it on high, but before he could bring it down, the hedge suddenly parted to let him through. Strange, he thought, and for a moment he was frightened. Only for a moment, though. Then he walked on.

As he passed through the hedge, he realized he could hear no birdsong, no dogs barking or cattle lowing or the impatient neighing of horses; he heard no laughter or chatter of people at work.

Very strange, he thought. He was no longer frightened but his curiosity grew with every step he took.

At last he came to the castle door. The guards on either side were fast asleep, snoring gently. If that had happened at his father's palace, they would have been dismissed at once. But he could not bring himself to be angry with them for, while they slept, he could enter the castle unchallenged.

Just inside stood a butler with a tray of cakes. The prince touched a cake and it crumbled into dust.

He walked past ladies-in-waiting who were waiting indeed, all fast asleep, their hands resting lightly in their laps. And near them their fine lords slumbered just as deeply. And the king — with his arm around the queen — snored gently on his throne.

Prince Florimund was astonished. He fancied he could almost hear the castle itself sleeping deeply, the stones moving in and out with each breath. He shook his head to clear away the fancy. But still he kept on until he came at last upon the girl he sought — Princess Aurora, asleep in the exact spot where she had fallen a hundred years before. In her sleep, she was as lovely as when he'd first beheld her, an apparition brought to him with the Lilac Fairy's magic.

Kneeling down by her side, he touched her cheek. It was warm beneath his fingers. He bent over and kissed her on the lips and her eyelids fluttered. When they opened, he nearly drowned in the blue depths of her eyes.

"You," she whispered.

"You," he answered.

It was a pledge.

The castle awoke at once, the stones no longer dreaming. King and queen and vizier, the little maids, and ladies and gentlemen, the snoring guards and gardeners, butlers and builders, cooks and coachmen — all woke up.

In no time at all, they turned the old birthday party into a wedding celebration. As at the christening so many years before, fairies fluttered in, their gossamer gowns shining with gold and silver and precious gems.

"You," whispered Florimund to Aurora, "are the most precious jewel of all."

Then, with the fairies' approval, all the heroes and heroines of fairy tale came to call. First to arrive was Puss in Boots with his partner, the White Cat. Next came Princess Florine, all in blue, and with her the Bluebird of Happiness. Red Riding Hood raced in, chased by the wicked wolf, followed by Hop-o-My-Thumb and his brother escaping the troll. Then came Cinderella and her prince, and the Fairy of Diamonds.

At last the music began to play for the prince and princess alone and they danced before their guests, who laughed and applauded with delight. "Because," as the Lilac Fairy said to the king and queen, as they watched the couple spin around and around, "these two will, indeed, live happily ever after."

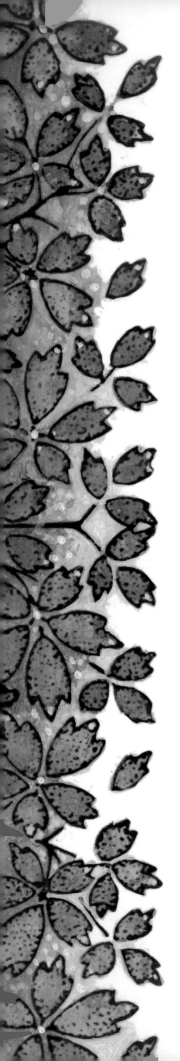

Daphnis and Chloe
INTRODUCTION

The story of Daphnis and Chloe is an ancient one, believed to have been written by the Greek author Longus, around the second or third century AD. The story combines two popular types of writing of the period: the Greek romance novel and pastoral poetry.

The ancient Greeks also loved stories about their gods. Pan, the half-human, half-goat son of the messenger god Hermes and the youngest of the immortals, plays an important part in this tale. Pan was the pipe-playing, mischief-making god of animals, shepherds, bee-keeping and music. He was said to chase nymphs through the forest and could turn nasty if awoken from his afternoon nap.

In the early twentieth century, many hundreds of years after the story of Daphnis and Chloe was written, it was made into a ballet for the Ballets Russes. Serge Diaghilev, the great Russian director who founded the Ballets Russes in 1911, was always looking for new ideas and the most talented people to work with. In fact, artists who designed sets for his ballets included the now world-famous painters Picasso and Matisse. Because Diaghilev's choreographer Michel Fokine was very keen to adapt a story from ancient Greece, Diaghilev decided to stage a ballet based on the tale of Daphnis and Chloe. He commissioned French composer Maurice Ravel to create the score.

The story has been changed so drastically that only one original adventure remains, although even this is quite altered. In the ballet, Chloe is captured by pirates in an exciting dance, whereas in the story it is Daphnis who is captured by pirates and saved by Chloe with the aid of the cowherd Dorcon (by contrast, an unsympathetic character in the ballet). In fact, in the original story Dorcon plays his pipes to direct his herd of cattle into the sea, creating a wave that overturns the pirate ship, allowing Daphnis to ride safely ashore straddling the backs of two cows. Clearly this part of the adventure could not be easily adapted for a ballet!

Creating the ballet was slow going, taking three years to complete. The work was complicated by the fact that Ravel and Fokine, who was Russian, did not speak the same language. Further complications arose when Fokine and the dancer playing Daphnis disagreed on how to portray the character. The premier was almost canceled as a result, but finally, on 8 June 1912, *Daphnis and Chloe* opened at the Théâtre du Châtelet in Paris. Audiences did not fully appreciate the ballet at the time. But it has continued to be staged and is now widely considered to be Ravel's masterpiece.

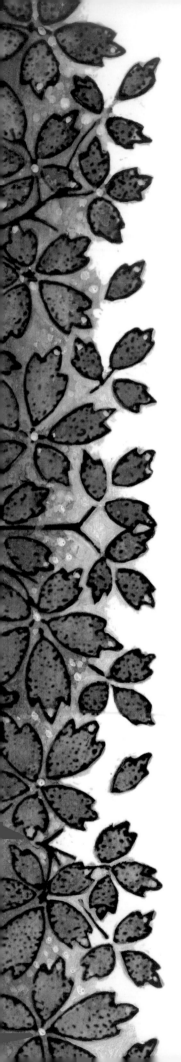

Daphnis and Chloe

ONCE UPON A TIME in ancient Greece, when the gods still ruled from high
Olympus, there was a lovely grotto dedicated to the forest god, Pan. A marble temple
stood in the heart of the grove of trees, guarded day and night by stone nymphs.

Now the day this story begins, all was quiet in the grotto. A small wind pushed
through the birch trees and brushed past the statues of the nymphs, but otherwise a
lovely stillness filled the grove.

Suddenly, as if wakening to the fact that it was a day of worship, thrush, wren and
cuckoo all began to sing. Their dawn chorus filled the grotto, little hymns to the
goat-footed god. Then into the grove came Pan's worshippers, young men and
women in white tunics, each carrying a basket of fruit and grain for Pan and the
stone nymphs. They were led by the grizzled old shepherd, Lammon, who had long
taken care of the grove.

The loveliest of all the worshippers was a young woman named Chloe. It was her
first time at Pan's temple, and she seemed to shine with the wonder of it, her dark
hair framing an exquisite oval face.

All the young men noticed her, but especially the cowherd, Dorcon. A big man
with a dark beard and a large jaw, he was rough and forward and had no sense of
what was proper. Besides, he'd been sampling the honey wine before pouring out a
libation to Pan. Grabbing Chloe by the arms, he tried to kiss her.

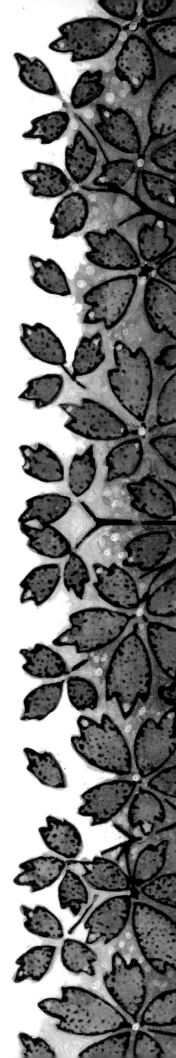

Chloe was so frightened, she cried out and struggled to break free. Suddenly Dorcon was thrown to the ground.

"The girl does not want your attentions," said Chloe's rescuer.

Gazing at him from under lowered lids, Chloe whispered, "Thank you, kind sir."

He blushed in return. "Not sir, but Daphnis. My name is Daphnis."

"Then thank you, Daphnis."

But from the ground, Dorcon persisted. "What's wrong with me, pretty girl? Why not thank me?" He started to rise.

Chloe shrank back from him, looking first at the handsome Daphnis, then at the other men for protection.

"A contest! A contest!" the men all cried.

Daphnis quickly took the lead. "Dorcon and I will dance before you and the best dancer will win a kiss from you," he suggested. "But say no if you do not agree and I will make sure that the others all abide by your wishes." He spoke so prettily, the color rising in his face again, that Chloe reluctantly agreed. It seemed the best way to get them all to leave her alone.

First Dorcon danced, but the drink had made him stupid and slow. He lumbered through his steps, missing several, almost falling. Everyone laughed at him. Then Daphnis began, and every step and turn he took seemed like a miracle. Yet he was the only one who was unaware of how well he danced. When he finished, the men hoisted him on to their shoulders, crying out, "The winner!" Then they set him down in front of Chloe. "The kiss! The kiss!"

Daphnis whispered to her, "Only if you wish it …" His breath was sweet-smelling, like wild flowers after rain. "I will not take what is not freely given, no matter how many contests I win."

She leaned toward him and closed her eyes, and the kiss they exchanged was — in all the universe of kisses — perfection.

Then, still mesmerized by the kiss, Chloe allowed herself to be led away deeper into the grove by the other girls so she might place her basket in Pan's temple.

Meanwhile, Daphnis stood without moving, as if the kiss had changed him to stone. A touch on his arm seemed to wake him, and he turned, expecting Chloe. But it was another woman, Lycaenion, older and with a calculating look on her face.

"Give me a kiss as well," she said.

71

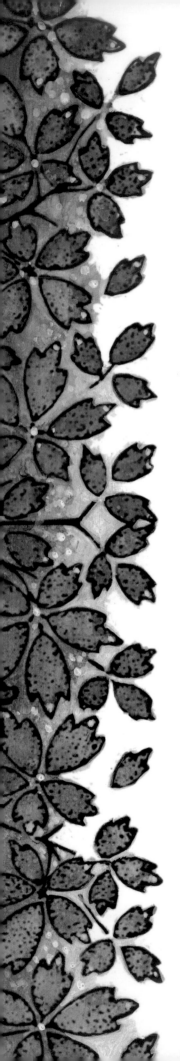

Appalled and blushing furiously, Daphnis dashed away, searching for Chloe. But, as fate would have it, he went in the wrong direction. And Lycaenion, shamed by Daphnis's rejection, left by another path.

For a moment, the grove was empty and silent, as if it, too, was remembering that perfect kiss. No birds, no bees, no little animals scrabbling in the undergrowth disturbed the peace. Even the girls in Pan's temple were silent at their prayers.

All of a sudden, the grove's silence was shattered by shouts and laughter, by grunts and belches and sharp whistles. Into that peaceful place raced a band of pirates dressed in striped trousers, with bared chests and colorful headscarves. They carried knives and swords shoved into their belts.

"Catch the girls!" shouted one. "That pretty maid and that one!" He pointed at two trembling young women hiding behind the trees.

As directed, the pirates chased after the girls, who raced through the grove like young deer ahead of a pack of wolves. Fear drove them, and they ran with the wind at their backs, till they had all escaped.

All, that is, but one. Surprised by the commotion around her — for she had no idea such wickedness existed — Chloe was caught, lifted up, carried off, all the while crying out to the gods to save her.

But the gods did not hear her. Or, if they did, they saved but a sandal from her foot. It lay on the ground where it had fallen, right by Pan's temple.

Just then, hearing Chloe cry out, Daphnis raced back into the grove. But too late — alas — too late. Seeing Chloe's sandal lying on the ground, he picked it up and held it to his heart.

"Oh, ye gods," he cried out, "those of you who heard my darling cry and would not save her, I curse you! I curse myself for being so slow!"

A sound in the grove startled him and he looked around. With a mighty wrenching of stone from stone, the nymphs of the grotto stepped down from their marble plinths, woodbine and ivy trailing through their fingers. They approached Daphnis, shaking their carved heads, and the sound was again the grinding of stone on stone.

"Do not curse the gods," they said in chorus. "It angers them very much."

"I do not care if the gods are angry," cried Daphnis. "Where is Chloe?"

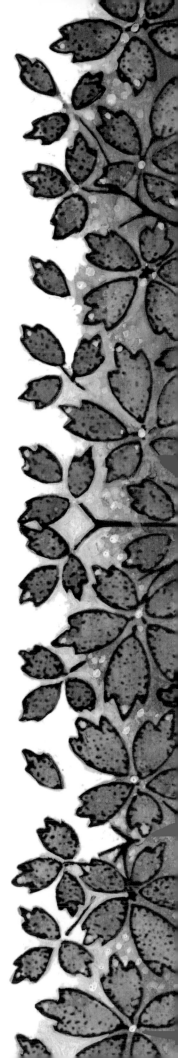

The stone nymphs spoke without moving their lips. "Pirates have stolen Chloe and taken her far away. You must ask the gods for help."

"Where were the gods when she was taken?" Daphnis said bitterly. "Why did they not help then?"

"Ah, but they *will* help," came the stone voices, "though in their own time, if you but temper your anger."

They pressed him to kneel, stone hands heavy on his shoulders. He got down on his knees, reluctantly, holding out Chloe's sandal to them.

"Ask the god of the grove and he *will* answer," the nymphs insisted in their voices of grating stone. "When the pirates stole away your true love, they violated Pan's sanctuary as well. He has no fondness for such men."

"Pan, help me," cried Daphnis, the memory of the perfect kiss still imprinted on his mouth. He trembled as he spoke, close to tears.

And Pan — who sees everything in his woods — heard him, though it would be some time before Daphnis was to understand this.

Meanwhile, Chloe had been carried off to the pirates' camp, a rough place with tables and benches made of driftwood and a black pirate flag hanging from a stunted tree. Hands bound tightly behind her, she was dragged before the chief pirate, the wicked Bryaxis.

Bryaxis was a great brute of a man, muscular and smelly. He smiled a serpent's smile when he saw Chloe, and stroked his large, dark moustache. "Can she dance?" he asked his men.

"Dance! Dance! Dance!" they shouted, as one took out his knife and cut the ropes binding Chloe's wrists.

With her hands free, Chloe dared to dream of escape. A small dream, but her first moment of hope. If I take long enough, she thought, perhaps they will drink too much to care about me and then I can run off. So she began to dance as ordered, to keep the pirates from guessing what she planned.

Slowly, languidly, Chloe moved about the encampment. As she danced, she watched the pirates. Her plan was working. The wine had made them sleepy and Bryaxis was already snoring. Several other pirates began to nod off, then several more. Making a final circuit around the rough camp, Chloe judged the moment to be right. She took a deep breath, gave thanks to the gods and made a dash for freedom.

But just as she reached the trail, her way was blocked by two huge pirates who had been standing guard behind the trees. "Oh, no!" she cried.

"Oh, yes!" they mocked her, grabbing her arms and dragging her back to Bryaxis, who had not been so drunk after all.

He laughed uproariously at her. "I did not say 'dash,' I said 'dance,' little one," he growled. "And dance you shall!"

Head down, spirit broken, she began to dance once more. Left foot, right foot, turn, and turn again, all the while whispering, "Pan, god of the groves, only let me see Daphnis one last time."

But that was a forlorn hope, for just then Bryaxis picked her up and held her triumphantly over his head. "No more dancing, no more prayers," he said, and laughed again.

"Pan, save me!" Chloe cried. And then she screamed, for, above her, lights had begun flickering in the sky, as if the heavens were opening to take her in. She turned her head

away from the lights and all at once hope leaped inside her. What she had spotted were the tall forms of the stone nymphs slowly, inexorably approaching the pirates' camp.

"Thank you, Pan," she whispered.

Thunder rattled the encampment, the very earth began to shake. And at that very moment, a great shadow — part man, part beast — seemed to fill the air.

Bryaxis threw her to the ground. "The goat-god is here. Pan the confuser. To the boats, men." he cried. "Poseidon, god of the sea, will see us safe."

In great panic — for that is what the god Pan inspires in men he hates — the pirates fled the clearing.

And Chloe blessed the ground with her tears.

In Pan's grotto, dread night gave way to dawn at last, but Daphnis still lay upon the ground mourning. He did not hear the birds singing or the laughter of shepherds around him. All he heard in his head were Chloe's last cries before the pirates took her. And the gods' silence.

"Wake up, wake up, Daphnis." A hand shook him roughly. Shepherds with their flocks had gathered around him.

"I have nothing to wake up for," he muttered, opening his eyes to the sunlight. The stone nymphs on the marble plinths stared down at him. He thought they were smiling. It did not comfort him.

The shepherds cried out, "Look! Look!"

He looked. And there was Chloe, coming along the path, surrounded by all her friends.

Daphnis could hardly believe his eyes. But hope lifted him up, and he ran to her, enfolding her in his arms.

Old Lammon came over and said softly, "Pan saved Chloe because he, too, once had a lost love, the nymph Syrinx. If you wish to honor the god who has bestowed such a gift, come to his altar and exchange your marriage vows there."

"I will honor Pan all my life," Daphnis exclaimed, "and never again doubt the gods." Then, taking Chloe by the hand, he led her to the little marble temple where they pledged themselves one to the other. As they spoke their vows, the stone nymphs smiled down on them. And Pan — who loves happy endings — granted them long, long lives of contentment ever after.

75

A Brief History of Classical Ballet

1581 *Le Ballet Comique de la Reine* ("The Comic Ballet of the Queen") is staged at the French court. It was commissioned by the queen, Catherine de Medici, who took part in it herself. Combining music, dance and a story, it was considered to be the first real ballet.

1661 King Louis XIV of France founds the Royal Academy of Dance in Paris and the first ballet to be performed in a series of scenes, like a play, is staged. Soon a school is established to train professional dancers — previously ballets were performed by courtiers and members of the nobility.

1726 Marie Camargo makes her Paris debut and shocks audiences by shortening her skirts to show off her leaps, unusually high for the time. Dancers were now more skilled technically and ballet was becoming more acrobatic.

1789 *La Fille Mal Gardée* ("The Badly Guarded Daughter") is staged in France, the first ballet to portray real people and everyday life. Country scenes and steps inspired by folk dancing were included in ballet from now on.

1832 *La Sylphide* is the first Romantic ballet to be performed, with the greatest ballerina of the time, Marie Taglioni — the first ballerina to dance *en pointe* — taking the lead. Ballets from this period were becoming more expressive, usually based on sad stories about ghosts or spirits. Ballerinas wore calf-length dresses and tights, which were introduced in about 1810.

1870 Marius Petipa takes over as director of the Imperial Russian Ballet and helps to develop a new kind of ballet, with choreographer and composer working much more closely together. Three or four acts long, these ballets were designed to show off the technical skill of the dancers, each act built around a *pas de deux* and solos for the leading male and female dancers.

On 25 May, *Coppélia*, with music by Léo Delibes and choreography by Arthur Saint-Léon, opens at the Paris Opera.

1877 On 4 March, *Swan Lake*, with music by Peter Ilyich Tchaikovsky and choreography by J. W. Reisinger, is staged for the first time at the Moscow Imperial Bolshoi Theatre but is considered a failure. Only after Marius Petipa re-choreographed the ballet some years later, in 1893, did it become a success.

1890 On 15 January, *The Sleeping Beauty*, with music by Tchaikovsky and choreography by Petipa, opens at the Maryinsky Theatre in St Petersburg, Russia. Highly successful both then and now, it came to be regarded as the high point of classical ballet.

1892 On 18 December, *The Nutcracker*, with music by Tchaikovsky and choreography by Petipa and Lev Ivanov, opens at the Maryinsky Theatre.

1909 *Les Sylphides*, with choreography by Michel Fokine and set to music by Frédéric Chopin, is the first "theme" ballet — a ballet with no story — to be staged. The early twentieth century saw a move away from technical brilliance for its own sake, with design and music playing an increasingly important part. From this time onward, while story ballets were still created, ballets were also based on more abstract themes.

1911 The Ballets Russes is founded by the great Russian director Serge Diaghilev and, with its bold and often shocking productions, dominates the ballet world for the next twenty years. Two of the greatest dancers of all time, Anna Pavlova and Vaslav Nijinsky, performed for the company.

1912 On 8 June, *Daphnis and Chloe*, performed by the Ballets Russes with music by Maurice Ravel and choreography by Michel Fokine, opens at the Théatre du Châtelet in Paris.

1931 The Vic-Wells Ballet is founded in London, directed by Ninette de Valois and with Frederick Ashton as resident choreographer. This was the company that eventually became the world-famous Royal Ballet.

1934 The School of American Ballet is founded, directed by Lincoln Kirstein and George Balanchine, one of the most influential choreographers of the twentieth century. He took classical ballet to its limits, making it faster and freer, and helped to bring it to a much wider audience.

1935 Under Communist rule in Russia, the Imperial Russian Ballet becomes the Kirov Ballet. It remains one of the foremost ballet companies of the world and has produced some celebrated dancers, including Rudolf Nureyev and Mikhail Baryshnikov, both of whom defected to the West.

1945 On 15 November, *Cinderella*, with music by Sergei Prokofiev and choreography by Rostilav Zakharov, is staged at the Bolshoi Theatre in Moscow.

Bibliography

BOOKS

Balanchine, George and Francis Mason, *101 Stories of the Great Ballets*, Anchor Books, Doubleday, New York, 1975, pp. 49–65, 277–83, 433–59

Grigorovich, Yuri and Victor V. Vanslov, *The Authorized Bolshoi Ballet Book of Sleeping Beauty* (translated by Yuri S. Shirokov), T.F.H. Publications, Neptune City, NJ, in association with VAAP Copyright Agency of the Soviet Union, 1987, pp. 13–30

Kerslet, Leo and Janet Sinclair, *A Dictionary of Ballet Terms*, Pitman Publishing Corporation, New York, 1957, pp. 66–7

Lifar, Serge, *A History of Russian Ballet: From its Origins to the Present Day*, Hutchinson & Co., London, 1954, pp. 140–3

Manchester, P. W. and Iris Morley, *The Rose and the Star: Ballet in England and Russia Compared*, Victor Gollancz, London, 1949, p. 57

Reynolds, Nancy and Susan Reimer-Torn, *Dance Classics: A Viewer's Guide to the Best-Loved Ballets and Modern Dances*, A Cappella Books, Pennington, NJ, 1991, pp. 31–50, 66–73, 81–4

Robert, Grace, *The Borzoi Book of Ballets*, Alfred A. Knopf, New York, 1946, pp. 76–9, 84–94, 280–316

Volkov, Solomon, *Balanchine's Tchaikovsky: Interviews with George Balanchine*, Simon and Schuster, New York, 1985, pp. 143–93

Zipes, Jack (ed.), *The Oxford Companion to Fairy Tales*, Oxford University Press, NY, 2000, pp. 239–40

BROCHURES

San Francisco Ballet: Facts. 100 Years of 'Beauty': An Annotated Chronology 1890–1990, San Francisco, CA

WEBSITES

(The subject or title of the webpage follows the website address; the date the site was accessed by the authors is given in brackets.)

www.artandculture.com/arts/artist?artistId=1297, Anna Pavlova (25.4.03)

www.artslynx.org/dance/beauty.htm, A *Sleeping Beauty* Timeline (25.4.03)

www.balletalert.com/ballets/Petipa/Sleeping%20Beauty/sleeping.htm, Ballet Alert! *Sleeping Beauty* (25.4.03)

www.ballet.co.uk/contexts/cinderella.htm, Ashton's *Cinderella* (14.4.03)

www.ballet.co.uk/contexts/nutcracker.htm, Ballet Contexts, *The Nutcracker* (17.4.03)

www.balletmet.org/Notes?SwanHist.html#anchor5399113, The Origins of *Swan Lake* (27.4.03)

www.ballet.org.uk/reference/notes/cinderella/index.html, *Cinderella* (14.4.03)

www.cmi.univ-mrs.fr/~esouche/dance/Daphnis.html, *Daphnis et Chloé* (1.5.03)

www.ballet.org.uk/reference/notes/sleepingbeauty/composer.html, English National Ballet, Ballet Reference: Production Notes. Tchaikovsky and the Creation of *The Sleeping Beauty* (25.4.03)

www.danceharrisonstreet.org/chor.html, Adrienne Dellas-Thornton (7.8.03)

www.dancer.com/Pavlova.html, Anna Pavlova (25.4.03)

www.kirjasto.sci.fi/hoffman.htm, E(rnst) T(heodor) A(madeus) Wilhelm Hoffmann (1776–1822) (7.3.03)

www.littlebluelight.com/lblphp/intro.php?name=Hoffmann, E. T. A. Hoffmann (7.3.03)

www.lugodoc.demon.co.uk/pan.htm, The Great God Pan (3.5.03)

www.music.indiana.edu/som/ballet/precollege/previewguide.html, Ravel's *Daphnis and Chloe* (11.3.03)

www.naxos.com/composer/ravel.htm, Ravel, Maurice (1875–1937) (1.5.03)

www.npr.org/programs/pt/features/daphnisandchloe.html, Performance Today: *Daphnis and Chloe* (1.5.03)

www.okcphilharmonic.org/c4_notes.html, "Classics 4 Program Notes" by Steven Ledbetter (1.5.03)

people.uncw.edu/deagona/ancientnovel/longus.htm, Longus: Daphnis and Chloe (1.5.03)

www.rickross.com/reference/unif/unif97.html, "Moon and his Ballet Stars" by Robert Black, *Telegraph*, 26 October 2000 (7.8.03)

www.rickross.com/reference/unif/unif140.html, "Universal Ballet's Really Big Show" by Sarah Kaufmann, *Washington Post*, 15 June 2001 (7.8.03)

www.soundventure.com/web/footnotes/episode1.html, *Swan Lake* (25.4.03)

www.soundventure.com/web/footnotes/episode3.html, *The Sleeping Beauty* (25.4.03)

www.soundventure.com/web/footnotes/episode8.html, *Cinderella* (14.4.03)

www.universalballet.co.kr/english/intro/purpose.html, Universal Ballet: Introduction (1.10.03)

Barefoot Books
Celebrating Art and Story

At Barefoot Books, we celebrate art and story that opens
the hearts and minds of children from all walks of life, inspiring
them to read deeper, search further, and explore their own creative gifts.
Taking our inspiration from many different cultures, we focus on themes that
encourage independence of spirit, enthusiasm for learning, and sharing of
the world's diversity. Interactive, playful and beautiful, our products
combine the best of the present with the best of the past to
educate our children as the caretakers of tomorrow.

Live Barefoot!
Join us at www.barefootbooks.com

Juliet Stevenson

is a stage and screen actress with many credits to her name, including *Truly, Madly, Deeply*; *Emma*; *Bend It Like Beckham* and *Mona Lisa Smile*. She was awarded the Laurence Olivier Award for Best Actress for her role in *Death and the Maiden*.

Jane Yolen and daughter Heidi E. Y. Stemple both took ballet as children. Jane studied for eight years with Balanchine's School of American Ballet, and afterward in Westport, Connecticut. Heidi only lasted a couple of years in ballet before switching to gymnastics. Now, Heidi's daughter Maddison is the ballerina of the family, dancing with Amherst Ballet in western Massachusetts where they all live. Jane and Heidi have written a dozen books together, including *Sleep, Black Bear, Sleep*, the *Unsolved Mysteries from History* series, *Dear Mother/Dear Daughter*, *Fairy Tale Feasts*, and the upcoming *The Barefoot Book of Dance Stories*.

Rebecca Guay graduated from the Pratt Institute in New York City with a degree in illustration. Rebecca is best known for her painted graphic novels for DC Comics and her illustrations for the card game *Magic: The Gathering*. Rebecca has also created book covers for young adult novels, illustrating the works of renowned writers Bruce Coville and Ursula K. LeGuin. Rebecca lives in Amherst, Massachusetts with her husband and daughter.